AMIAYA ENTERTAINMENT LLC
Presents

SO MANY TEARS

A NOVEL

by

Teresa Aviles

Copyright ©2005 by Teresa Aviles
Written by Teresa Aviles for Amiaya Entertainment LLC

Published by Amiaya Entertainment LLC

Cover design by Marion Designs

Edited by Antoine "Inch" Thomas

Printed in the United States

ISBN: 0-9745075-9-8

[1. Urban — Non-Fiction 2. Drama — Non-Fiction 3. New York City — Non-Fiction]

ACKNOWLEDGEMENTS

After thanking God, First and foremost I would like to thank my parents Mildred and Ernest Hill who gave me life. And then I would like to thank Hector E. Aviles, with whose teenage love and lust I managed to produce the best son a mother and father could hope for. Second, I would like to thank the siblings that came along after Isidro. Peanut, who was so close to Isidro that they became like twins. Sanyae, who when speeding down the streets and highways of the city, constantly reminds me that it was her big brother who taught her how to drive. Ricky, who grew up to idolize Isidro. I remember the day we brought you from the hospital. Your brother took you in his arms and proudly said, *"I want to carry him in the building because I have been waiting for this day for fifteen (15) years."* I will remember the smile on his face for all of my days on earth. I would also like to thank the special friends that made life bearable during the darkest days of my life. They are too many to mention individually, but I would like to give special thanks to Lts. Richard Evans and Joe Blanck, Police Officers Trellis Jones and Dwayne Davis and Det. Doug Davis. Trellis, without your help I would have probably still been wandering the streets of Rochester, Minnesota or perhaps in some mental ward as an unidentified EDP, (emotionally disturbed person). To my friend, Frances Brunson, thank you for taking my hand and bringing me back to life. Thank you, Ricky, for sending Frances to help me. And also, I would like to thank my friends and fellow drug war warriors who continue to fight the cruel, inhumane, unjust, racist and costly war on drugs: Nora

Callahan, Chuck Armsbury and, may he rest in peace, Mark Harrison of the *November Coalition*, Randy Credico, Tony Papa, Regina Stevens, Elaine Bartlett, Sara and Emily Kunstler, Margaret Ratner Kunstler, Nazimova Varick and Evelyn Sanchez of *Mother's of the New York Disappeared*. And, to my very special friend who has become a brother to me and who befriended me and showed me love and compassion during the darkest days of my life, Paul Bennett. If there were more people in the world like you, there would be no war on drugs. And last but not least, Mr. Antoine Thomas, who took a chance on me when no one else would.

DEDICATION

This book is dedicated to my Angel, my first-born son, Isidro laMont Aviles, whose fond memory is the driving force in my life. My son, your passing has shattered my heart into little pieces that were slowly chipped away and there is now a hole in the place where my heart used to be. You will live on forever in my heart and you will always be the jewel in the crown of my life. Rest in peace, my son.

Love, Mother

"DON'T GET THROWN ON THE SHIP"

Are you one of those people who are so far into your comfort zone that you think that slavery has been abolished? Well, let me tell you, slavery is alive and well here in these United States of America, and if you are not very careful, you will find out the hard way. Let's do a little comparison... Hundreds of years ago there were slave catchers. They would travel to Africa, take to the bush and hunt down unsuspecting Africans who would be put into chains and thrown into the bowels of the slave ship and brought to America to work for free on the plantations. Today there are different kinds of "slave catchers" who come disguised as police officers, DEA agents, FBI agents, lawyers and judges, but their goal is the same as the old time slave catchers and that is to provide free labor in this country. Instead of being thrown into the bowels of the slave ships, these modern day slaves are thrown into the belly of the beast. Instead of spending months in the bowels of a slave ship, the new slaves spend time in kangaroo courts that are designed to make it look like they are getting a fair trial and that they are being judged by an impartial group of their peers. Just think back on any criminal court case that you sat in on, whether it was State or Federal.

Have you ever seen anyone of your friends or relatives judged by a group of their peers? The new plantations are disguised as Federal or State Correctional Institutions. They are almost always located in some remote part of the state where there was not even a McDonald's Restaurant until the correctional facility came to town. If you drive through certain parts of any state in this country, you can tell immediately if there is a prison complex somewhere nearby. All you have to do is look at the houses and you will know. You will usually see some broken down, ramshackled house, badly in need of a new front porch and a fresh coat of paint. You will see many of these houses as you drive along the countryside and then out of the blue, up pops a large brick house with a neatly manicured lawn, a pool in the back yard and a new car in the driveway. You know immediately that there is a prison in this town and that one or more persons in the family that owns this house works for the prison.

Now what do you think goes on behind these prison walls while our family members are being corrected. I bet some of you think that they are sitting there watching color TV, lifting weights or going to college. Well, think again. These prisoners are working, working hard and for little or nothing. They are not making license plates. They are making clothing and furniture for the military. They are making goods that are contracted out by companies who, instead of paying the minimum wage, are paying these prisoners NOTHING. So, it is not by accident that these "new slave catchers" are coming into our neighborhoods and snatching up the slaves and putting them on the "New Slave Ship." It is all a part of a well-orchestrated plan. I bet another thing you did not know is that while these "slaves" are being warehoused in these countryside complexes, that they are not being counted as part of the census from the urban city from which they came, but they are being counted as part of the census of the town in which they are imprisoned, thereby providing not only good paying jobs for otherwise unemployable persons, but tax dollars for that community as well. So, the next time you drive your expensive car into your driveway, in your middle-class neighborhood, go inside and take off your brand named clothing and sit down in front of your big screen TV and kick back in the comfort zone to which you have become accustomed. Just be aware that you too could become a candidate for the NEW SLAVE SHIP. In order to stay off of the new slave ship, there are certain things that you must avoid. The first is to not hang around on corners talking, drinking beer and smoking a blunt. The second is especially for young black males. Do not travel in groups. When there are two or three young black males traveling together, they are sure to fit the description of a robbery suspect. Try traveling alone and avoid wearing the young black man's uniform, which is made up of baggy jeans and the long white tee shirt. Your chances of getting stopped by the police become less if you are wearing a pair of khakis and a button down shirt. The same holds true for those of you driving in your cars. Don't drive around blasting your music and bobbing your bandana-clad head while you are in your expensive SUV. No matter how hard you worked for it, you are better off if you don't tint the windows or blast music. Also, make sure that your taillights are in good working order. A Broken Tail Light is always a good reason for the cops to pull you over. AND, last but not least, the best way to stay off of the ship is not to accept telephone calls from your so-called friends in prison. Remember, they are tired of being on the ship and would do anything to shorten their time on the ship, including SNITCH on you, isn't that right, Mr. Joe Rat?

In loving memory of
Isidro laMont Aviles
1964 – 1998

PROLOGUE

BRIGHT, SUNNY DAYS

Bright sunny days always remind me of my firstborn son, Isidro (pronounced See-Dro) laMont Aviles. He was born on a bright sunny Saturday at 3 o'clock in the afternoon of October 10, 1964. I can remember my thoughts the first time I looked down into his beautiful face. My first thought was, *"Gosh, he does not look at all like me, but like a miniature version of his father."* Of course, this was long before the phrase "Mini-Me" was coined. My second thought was that I loved him instantly and I looked into his face and promised to always love him and be there for him, no matter what. Who would know then, that at the time in his life when he needed me the most, I would be nowhere around. I am writing this book in memory of my loving son, Isidro laMont Aviles, who lost his life due to this country's cruel, inhumane, ineffective and expensive War on Drugs. Rest in peace, my son, and remember that I will always love you. *Mom*

CHAPTER ONE

DECEMBER 12, 1990

It was a cloudy day when I returned home from work and all I could think of was getting in the house, taking off my shoes and lying down for a while before I had to cook dinner. The sky was cloudy, the day was dreary and gloomy and, as I look back on it now, I can see that the day held the promise of impending doom. I took out my keys to open the door and before I had a chance to put the key in the keyhole, the door swung open. My youngest daughter, Sanyae, (pronounced San-yay) stood there with a look that I can only describe as destroyed. Her words still ring in my ear. "Ma, the FEDS got Isidro."

"What?" I dropped my bags to the floor and again said, "What?" as if saying it again was going to change what Sanyae just told me. I asked her what happened, when, how and why. She was standing there with Lessie, Isidro's expectant girlfriend who looked as bad as Sanyae did, and before she could answer me, the phone rang. I grabbed it off the hook and said, "Hello." It was my son, my firstborn child, Isidro. I asked him, "Isidro, what happened? Where are you? Are you okay?" Everything came out of my mouth so fast that Isidro almost didn't have a chance to answer. But I had to breath some air back into my lungs and that's when Isidro told me what happened.

"Ma, J.P. has gotten me in some deep shit," he said angrily. "But I should be good because the cops didn't find any drugs on me."

After hearing that, I felt immediate relief. We would go to court with him in the morning and when the judge hears that he had no drugs, he should be let go with instructions to appear in court at a later date.

My relief was short lived. After a long stressful night, we were up early and ready to go to court. The Feds had taken Sanyae's car from Isidro at the time of his arrest so we were forced to take public transportation.

I can just imagine how sneaky the cops were when they arrested him. They probably hit their flashers, sounded their loud speaker and said, "Pull over! Pull your car over! Shut your engine off and put your hands where I can see them!"

Isidro, never being one to disrespect, reluctantly complied. Then I can see the officer walking over to Isidro's car, pistol drawn and yelling, "Step outta the car now! Keep your hands where I can see 'em! Now lay on the ground and place your hands behind your head." As Isidro is doing what he's told, the racist cop is easing over top of Isidro, and right before he grabs Isidro's wrists to cuff him, the officer smiles a devilish grin, spits out some residue from the tobacco he's chewing, thinks to himself, *Another one bites the dust*, then handcuffs Isidro leaving no room for his arms to breathe.

The day got off to a bad start as soon as we entered the #2 downtown IRT train. It was raining outside and the train was overcrowded with umbrella toting riders who were just as eager to get where they were going as we were. Although we got on only three stops from the beginning of the line, there was no hope for getting a seat. We squeezed into the car like sardines in a can and were glad for the standing room. Some riders were even left standing on the platform to wait for the next train.

We went to Manhattan Federal Court in the Southern District of New York where everyone was crisp, businesslike and impolite. We asked for and were given instructions on how to find the court where Isidro's first of many hearings was held. When we got inside, there were only a couple of people sitting down, waiting for their names to be called. I sat and listened and it seemed that these hearings were moving along rather quickly when there was so much at stake. Suddenly, we heard that Isidro's case was being called next. Out of nowhere, several men and women in business suits appeared. Sanyae looked at me and asked, "Who are all of these people?" Sanyae knew I couldn't answer the question, but she was just wondering out loud. And because I was the closest one to her, she looked at me while she expressed her feelings.

I had no idea who they were, but it seemed as if something very important was about to take place. A shiesty looking lawyer, a Mr. AL Meyers stood up and said, "Your Honor, I'm here to represent Mr. Isidro laMont Aviles." The attorney fingered his files and waited for the judge's response.

My first thought was, *Who is he and where did he come from?* No one told us that Isidro had been appointed an attorney. As far as I was concerned, he did not need one, after all, he had no drugs when he was arrested.

The Assistant U.S. Attorney, whom I would later refer to as the devil's daughter, stood up and started rattling off the charges against Isidro. When she finished, it appeared that my son was someone from America's Most Wanted.

Where had they gotten this crap from? I was ready to jump out of my seat and say that they had the wrong person. I knew my son and I knew him well. For the first time in my life I began to feel like the air was being sucked out of my chest. I wanted to start screaming to the top of my lungs. I waited for that feeling you get when you wake up panting from a bad dream. Yeah, this had to be a dream, but it was taking me a very long time to wake up.

I must have blanked out for a minute because the next thing I knew I was hearing the words, *"...held without bail, dangerousness and risk of flight."* What the fuck were they talking about? Isidro was not dangerous and he certainly was not going anywhere. This is the shit you see on TV, this don't happen in real life. Isidro was held without bail. When I heard *no bail,* my mouth dropped open but no words would come out. There was a lot of rambling on about *dangerousness* and *risk of flight.* I watched helplessly as my son was led from the courtroom with his hands cuffed behind his back. I knew Isidro was sad, and probably mad as hell too. But Isidro was strong. He was born with a will to survive so however bad he was feeling, he wouldn't let his family witness it and he damn sure wouldn't give the courts the satisfaction. So with that, Isidro glanced over at us one quick time, gave a short, quick nod indicating that he'd be alright and for us not to worry.

Not to worry? At that point, *not to worry* became my middle name. And if at that point you could've actually *seen* my nerves, they would have reminded you of my son Ricky's room, *a mess.*

I wanted to reach out and grab Isidro. I wanted to snatch him from the federal agents, run from the courthouse and take him to a place where these mean spirited people could not get their hands on him ever again. The sight of a child being led away with his hands cuffed behind his back and being shoved along by some big burly white man is something that tears at the very fiber of a mother's being. I was devastated. I did not know what to do or what to say. Lessie remained silent while Sanyae began to sob uncontrollably. Out of fear and nervousness I yelled at her. I said, "Shut up, Sanyae!" Then I looked at her. My eyes were tight like a closed set of Venetian blinds. I tightened up my mouth and spoke to her nice and slowly as if she were a four-year-old. I said, "Lessie, if you don't stop that damn crying, I'm going to slap the shit out of you!"

Lessie cut her eyes at me and noticed how serious I was. After all the hollering she did, her mouth immediately closed and not another sound came out. Her body jerked once as if she had the hiccups and was holding it in, but when I turned toward her again and raised my hand, I think she stopped the blood from flowing through her body. She realized how real it was and shut right up. At that time, all I could think about was not making Isidro feel any worse than I knew he felt at that moment. Again, I began feeling like something was sucking the air out of my chest. I wanted to fall to my knees and cry, but I knew that I had to hold myself together so that I could help *ALL* of my children, the one who was being led away in handcuffs *and* the others who stood by watching helplessly. I can remember thinking that Lessie must've felt pretty bad too, although she did not show it, or maybe she did and I was too wrapped up in my own pain that I did not see it. She was young, having her first child and was probably in shock. Nobody gets held without bail in a drug case where there are no drugs! The United States government had stolen a jewel out of the crown of my life. Somehow we *had* to make it through the weekend.

CHAPTER TWO

We left the courtroom and approached the attorney who said that he was there to represent Isidro. All I had heard him say on my son's behalf was that he was waiving Isidro's right to a preliminary hearing. I did not know what a preliminary hearing was, but from what we had just witnessed, Isidro probably needed this hearing. It seemed that the U.S. attorney had done all the talking while this *Al Meyers* character stood by looking stupid. From the sound of it, *"preliminary hearing,"* I would think that this was where Isidro got to tell the judge what really happened. Boy was I the stupid one Mr. Meyers told us that he was not actually my son's attorney but was just standing in as a friend of the court. He damn sure was a friend of the court because he sure wasn't a friend to my son, *waiving his rights and all.* This should have been against the law. While we were there speaking to him, Isidro was brought from a back door in the courtroom and whisked down the hall to what I guess was a holding area. It really tore at my heart, seeing my son being led away with his hands cuffed behind him. It is a sight that no mother should ever have to witness.

Upon leaving the courthouse, I immediately headed

across town to my union hall. I was praying that they had some sort of help for us in their legal department. My hopes were dashed when we were told that they did not represent union members in legal matters. The legal department sent me downstairs to the Personal Service Unit to speak to a counselor. I had Sanyae wait outside for me and I went in alone to see the counselor. As soon as she approached me I began to cry uncontrollably. It seemed that things had been getting worse and worse as the day wore on. There was nothing that the counselor could do for us, but it was a brief relief to just have a sympathetic ear to listen to me and a shoulder to lean on if only for a few minutes. I only stayed with the counselor for a few minutes because we had to get over to Federal Plaza to see about the car. Although we had been told that the car was being seized for forfeiture because it had been used in drug trafficking, we were told to see an Agent Wiggins because he might be able to help us.

We got to 26 Federal Plaza and were told to go upstairs and ask for Agent Wisemann. After sitting for about twenty minutes, Agent Wisemann, the agent who had told us to ask for Agent Wiggins, came out to meet us. Sanyae asked him, "How come Agent Wiggins didn't come speak to us?" Sanyae was from the hood, but she had class with herself. But being around those agents and court officers all day and listening to *their* lingo and dialect made Sanyae seem ghetto.

Agent Wisemann noticed it too and became very annoyed at that point. He frowned up his face and in a sarcastic tone responded, "You want to wait for Agent Wiggins? Because if you do, I'll go back and let you wait."

I think if you looked up federal agent in the dictionary, a photo of Wisemann would be looking out at you. He looked at me first and I looked back at his ass like, *"Who the fuck do you think you're talking to?"*

Then he looked over at Sanyae who was about to explode.

I'm a little rough around the edges so I don't play that shit. I'm short, dark skinned, with a thick build. And I'm down for whatever. Sanyae, on the other hand, is the opposite of me.

Sanyae is brown skin, 5'6", slim, she has that uppity, educated, no nonsense approach and she's a little on the quiet side. But once you get her started, it's hard to calm her down. And, because I knew that we would need the car in the next few weeks, I told Sanyae to just cool it and let him handle it. It was very obvious that he did not like being challenged and that he was not used to being spoken back to. He stood over us, looking down at us as if he dared us to say another word. He was not a person who we wanted to cross, so we said we would take the car from him and leave. He told us to go downstairs and wait at the driveway in front of the garage which was located on the south side of the building at 26 Federal Plaza. As we had been doing all day, we did what we were told without asking any further questions. We took the elevator to the first floor and headed for the driveway to wait for Agent Wisemann.

The night was cold and a slight rain was falling. Not the kind that made you too wet, but the kind that just made you mad. We stood on the street in front of the driveway shivering from both the cold and the rain. We had been standing there for about twenty minutes and were beginning to wonder if we were ever going to get the car back when all of a sudden we saw lights coming from the underground garage. Agent Wisemann drove the car to where we were standing, put it in park, turned off the ignition and then got out of the car. He handed the keys to me and then walked away without another word or a backward glance. Sanyae and I were standing there dumbfounded. He had not asked us for a driver's license or any identification. I found this strange because when the police voucher a car, you have to produce a driver's license, vehicle registration and an insurance ID card before they even consider releasing the car to you. Then, you have to sign a form that states that the car was released to you. Agent Wisemann did none of this. He just gave the car keys to us and walked away. I was just glad that he gave the car back to us because he had said earlier that the car was being seized for forfeiture. We got in the car and headed north on the FDR Drive.

The day's events had taken its toll on Sanyae and I. Before we got into the car, I warned Sanyae to be careful about what she said *in* the car. I was paranoid because of the way that the car was returned to us. I sat down in the car and began looking for any recording devices. I felt that they had given the car back to us so they could gather some more evidence against Isidro. Instead of talking to Sanyae, I began to write notes to her, warning her not to say anything out loud that had anything to do with Isidro. We spoke about the weather and what we were going to have for dinner, but we did not mention a word about Isidro. After a while we stopped talking altogether and instead, sat out the ride in silence. When we got in front of our building, we both jumped out of the car at the same time. We were not used to taking such long rides in silence.

As soon as we got out of the car, we started discussing what we were going to tell Ricky, my youngest son, and Peanut, my daughter, about Isidro. It was easy to decide that we had to tell Ricky something right away because we did not want him to answer the phone and be told what was going on from someone else.

We sat Ricky down in the living room and I told him, "Honey, listen up." I grabbed him gently underneath his chin and turned his face so that we were eye to eye. Then, in the calmest voice said, "Ricky, Isidro got into a *little* trouble and now he's in jail." I looked at him wondering what he was thinking at that point. When his expression remained the same as if the sudden news had no effect on him, I continued while Ricky sat and listened intently. I explained exactly what had happened and told him that we were going to do everything in our power to bring him home as soon as possible.

The first question Ricky asked was, "Why did they take him to jail if he didn't have any drugs?"

We did not bother trying to explain the conspiracy laws to him because we were having a hard time understanding them ourselves. But we did make sure that Ricky knew not to discuss anything about Isidro with anyone. We did not have to tell Ricky this twice because he was very loyal to his brother and had always looked up to Isidro. Even though they were fifteen years apart, they had always been very close to one another.

Ricky was anxious to get back to his video games, but when he walked back towards his room, we could see the concern in his face. It was very painful to see an eleven-year-old having to worry about his brother being in jail. Living in a New York City housing project, you never know what Ricky had heard about jail in the past.

Deciding to tell Ricky was easy, but what to tell Peanut was another matter. She was five months pregnant and was stationed miles away from home in Spain. We did not want to tell her anything that would upset her. It seemed that every time she got pregnant, our family had a tragedy. She was eight months pregnant with her second child when my father passed away on Christmas day. She was very close to the person she referred to as *"her only grandfather in the whole world,"* and had barely gotten over his death and now we had to tell her that her older brother was in prison. We discussed this several times over the course of the next few days and decided that it would be best if we told her *after* she had the baby. We were successful in keeping this from her for a few weeks, but when Christmas came, she knew that something was wrong because she had not spoken to Isidro and she knew that there was something wrong if he was not home for Christmas. There was no beating around the bush, so we just came right out and told her what had happened. She immediately burst out in tears and it tore me apart not to be there to put my arms around her and tell her that everything was going to be okay. I kept her on the phone until she calmed down, but in the back of my mind I was wondering how I was going to pay for this long distance overseas call.

When Peanut finally calmed down, she said something that I could hear over and over in my head for years to come. Peanut said, "Ma, I just don't see a happy ending to this." Isidro and Peanut were only eighteen months apart in age and at times, were like twins. How could she know that the ending would not be good?

CHAPTER THREE

THE FIRST VISIT

We made plans to visit Isidro who had been taken to the Federal Correctional Institution in Otisville, New York. When I found out that he had been taken all the way up to Otisville, New York, I was enraged. *Why were they taking my son to a prison when he hadn't even had his day in court?* I thought of calling the news media to let them know what was going on because I could not believe that this was happening. I kept thinking that this was a bad dream and that I was going to wake up and the dream was going to fade from my memory. Little did I know that I was not going to wake up from this nightmare, but that it was going to last, *for the rest of my life.*

I was able to convince Steven to drive me to Otisville on Friday evening, the first visiting day that Isidro was allowed to have since his arrest. I so was excited about seeing Isidro and wanted everything to go smoothly. I needed to know that he was okay. I was worried if he was eating or sleeping.

I wanted to know if the staff was treating him right and if anyone was bothering him. I wanted to know if he was okay physically, but most of all, I needed to let him know that we loved him and that I would do everything in my power to bring him home. Because I was not used to traveling on the highway, I asked a family member, who is a correction officer, for directions. We got on the road and it was not until we had traveled one hundred miles in the wrong direction that we discovered that we were going south and we should have been going north. We turned around and broke all speed limits so that we would arrive at the institution before they closed off the visiting room.

We filled out the visiting forms and sat waiting impatiently to be called. I was sitting lost in thought when I heard my name being called. There are no words to describe how I felt when I was told that I could not visit my son because in my haste to get there I had forgotten my identification card at home. I was his *mother* and I had traveled miles to get there and I was *not* going to be turned away. I asked to speak to a supervisor, foolishly thinking that I could explain my predicament and that I would be allowed inside. This, too, was not to be. I was told, oh so politely, that I would not get in, under *any* circumstances, and that I could come back the next day. It's funny how that night prepared me for the years that lay ahead and for my many dealings with the Bureau of Prisons. I had always been under the impression that the hardest thing about going to visit someone in prison was getting there. It would take years before we had perfected the art of visiting an inmate, but after a while, we became experts at visiting the prisons. Over the years, every time I entered a prison, I thought of writing a book, *"The Art of Visiting a Loved One in Prison."* I still think about it sometimes too. Anyway, we turned around and headed back toward New York City, but the last few days finally caught up to me and I began to sob hysterically. The government had stolen my first-born child and thrown him into the belly of the beast. I had to leave the institution, but they had not heard the last of me.

CHAPTER FOUR

THE YOUNG ISIDRO

On the long ride home, my mind began to wander back to the days when my son was growing up. He was always a free spirit with a smile that brightened up my day. He was a curious little person who always wanted to know what made things work. Whenever he got a new toy, the first thing he wanted to do was to take it apart and find out what made it work. I remember once when my mother bought a bearskin rug, he seemed fascinated by it. He ran his little hands up and down the length of the rug and then asked thoughtfully, "Grandma, where is the hole?"

She asked, "What hole?"

He looked at her, amazed that she would ask such a silly question and said, indignantly, "The hole where they shot him." Of course, being Isidro, he kept feeling the rug until he found the hole and said proudly, "Here it is," and sure enough, when we looked closely, we could see the round hole.

One of his favorite toys when he was a young boy was *Johnny-Lightening* cars. He loved to see the cars racing around the track. After a while I began to love Johnny Lightening too. Especially when I discovered that the tracks were flexible and very good for whipping little butts.

When Isidro grew up, his love for fast cars remained and he added fast women to this hobby. He was handsome from the first day and, he was loved by many. He was the type of child who would carry packages for an old lady and refuse a tip.

One day he found a wallet that belonged to one of our neighbors. He was about maybe fourteen or fifteen years old at the time. He never mentioned the incident to me, but a few days after he returned the wallet to the lady, she stopped me in the elevator and told me how nice my son was and how he refused to take a tip after returning her wallet. She went on to say that she never thought she would get the wallet back with the two hundred and seventy-five dollars cash plus all of her credit cards and identification. I was proud that I had taught him well. I don't know if even I was that honest. The nuns in the catholic school could not resist his smile, even after he was caught taking a sip of the wine when he was an alter boy. When all else failed, he would always turn on that charming smile. Yes, Isidro was a bright and shining star.

Isidro went through school without any major problems. For a short time in grade school he was the class clown. One teacher told me that when she would turn her back to the class, they would always burst out in laughter, and when she turned around to face the class, she knew immediately that whatever happened had been caused by Isidro. When I asked her how she knew this, she replied, "Because he was the only one with a serious face and the other kids were all laughing hysterically." Isidro adjusted well to catholic school where I sent him after he seemed to be having trouble reading. It took me years to discover that he had a hard time with anything that did not interest him. He had to be held back his first year in catholic school, but did very well the second year. I suspect that it had something to do with being in the same class as his younger sister. Knowing Isidro, there was no way that he was going to let his sister get to high school before him, so he did what he had to do to graduate and move on to high school. Isidro did well in high school once he discovered the gymnastics team. He would often come home with painful blisters on his hands from the parallel bars, but he refused to give up. In fact once he set his mind to it, he never gave up on anything. He was good at whatever he did. One of his father's friends once said, "Man, you have the kind of son that every man dreams of having," and I agreed with him.

When Isidro was about eight years old, I registered him with the Fresh Air Fund so that my children could have a summer in the country. Isidro went to a quaint little town in upstate New Kingston, New York, for his first year. He spent two weeks with the *Squires* family. There were the parents, Spooky and Lois, three daughters, Tracy, Janet and Lisa, and one son, Warren. Warren and Isidro got along very well and spent a great summer together. They were like Tom Sawyer and Huckleberry Finn. They did all of the things that Isidro loved but did not get a chance to do living in the city. By the end of the two weeks, the family was sorry to let Isidro go and he was sad about having to leave. They loved Isidro and said that they were sorry that he could not stay longer than the two weeks that the Fresh Air Fund allowed for the first visit.

Warren and Isidro got along so well that the Squires invited Isidro back for the Christmas vacation. On December 26th, we drove to New Kingston for the first time so that Isidro could have a winter recess in the country. On the drive upstate, Isidro excitedly told us about all of the things that we could expect and was anxious to show us around. Of course I was a little apprehensive because I had never stayed overnight at a white person's house before. Before we even pulled up in the driveway, I saw why Isidro was so excited. The whole family was standing on the front porch ready to greet us. They were wonderful people and we all got along well.

We were sitting around their dining room table exchanging stories about country life versus city life while the kids all romped and played in the yard. My husband, *Hector*, as always, began to brag about my homestyle cooking which made the Squires become eager to try my fried chicken. Before the night was over, we had the whole town over for fried chicken and potato salad. Isidro went to visit the Squires family every summer for years and also on most of his vacations from school, but I will always remember that day when we sat around the dining room table eating fried chicken with everyone. Isidro seemed to be so proud of his mother's cooking and had a big smile on his face the entire evening. That was the first of many trips that our family took up to New Kingston to spend time with the Squires and each time they made us feel like part of their family. I will never forget the New Kingston Whoop Danny Do where everyone in town sets up tables on their front lawns to have a giant cook out. Little did we know on that day when everyone was so happy that neither Warren nor Isidro would live for very long.

CHAPTER FIVE

ISIDRO, THE YOUNG MAN

Shortly after high school, Isidro joined the Army and went off to Columbia, South Carolina, to begin his basic training. I drove to South Carolina for his graduation and my eyes welled up with tears upon seeing him in his dress uniform for the first time. He was so handsome, he looked like a poster boy for the US Army. Isidro was a disciplined person and was able to breeze through basic training and then went on to Fort Hood, Texas, where he completed some more intensive training. When his Army Reserve training was over, he headed home, a decision that was probably the beginning of the end.

Before long, Isidro was back in New York City and became father and husband, *in that order*. He was very proud of his baby girl, Sidra, who was named after him and rightly so. She looked like a miniature version of him. He loved his daughter and she loved him back and wherever he was, she wanted to be there too. Unfortunately, the *"baby's mama"* did not feel the same and chose to go a different way. Before long, Isidro had to become a *visiting* daddy, but that did not stop him from loving his daughter any less or *her* loving him.

One of the most special times in all of my life was the week I spent in Virginia with Isidro and Sidra. Isidro had gone down to Norfolk, Virginia, to visit his sister, Peanut, and decided to stay and make it home. Isidro came to New York to pick up his daughter so that she could spend some time with him and decided to take his little brother Ricky back with them. My cousin Tuti and I decided that we would go down there to bring the children back and also have a little *R&R* too. I think I can say that it was the most special time in all of my life. When I think about that week, it always brings back the fondest memories. We arrived in Virginia on Friday night and spent the evening talking about old times and eating take out food. We talked and laughed into the wee hours of the morning until we passed out. My daughter, Peanut, also joined us with her husband, Don, and her two daughters, Donya and Donyae. There were so many of us in the house that we had to use air mattresses and sleeping bags, but we were with loved ones so it did not matter. What mattered was that we were all together.

The next morning we got up bright and early and prepared to go out on the town. After we were all fed, bathed and dressed, we headed for the hills, *so to speak*. Isidro grabbed his diving gear and we went down to Virginia Beach where we had a fantastic time. The kids splashed in the clear blue waters of Virginia Beach while Isidro went scuba diving in the waters. He had a crowd on the beach asking questions about the diving gear, which was just like Isidro, *he had a crowd wherever he went*. The children were especially proud that *"Daddy," "Big Brother"* and *"Uncle Isidro"* was getting so much attention.

After spending the day on the beach, we headed back to Norfolk for a nice dinner and a quiet evening at home in front of the television. The children were exhausted and fell asleep immediately after getting out of the bathtub, and again we had one of our *"remember when"* all-nighters. We spent the next few days going up and down the Virginia highways. One day we went to Kings Dominion, a trip I will never forget for the rest of my life. We all went into the park and immediately everyone wanted to go in a different direction. Since I was still a little worn out from the past few days, I decided to take a seat and let everyone know that this was our *"point"* and that anyone who needed anything was to come back to the *point.* Isidro, Tuti and Ricky ran to play the games that gave the biggest prizes and Isidro, being the sportsman that he was, started winning huge stuffed animals right away. Each time he won one, he would bring it back to me and be off again. Before long, I was sitting down surrounded by about ten *HUGE* stuffed animals. People were walking by staring at me in wonder. While sitting there, one of Isidro's friends decided that she was going to take the children to the merry-go-round. I was sitting there in the heat when they came back and I said to myself as I saw them walking toward me, *"There is something wrong with this picture."* Marie left with two children and only came back with *ONE.*

"Where is my other granddaughter?" I yelled out to Marie.

She looked down at her empty hand and, in her country bumpkin drawl said, "Oh, the little girl, she just upped and walked away from me!"

It was at that moment that I knew I was capable of murder. "What the FUCK do you mean she just upped and walked away from you? Where the hell is she?" I jumped up from my spot in the sun and ran towards Lord knows where. A million thoughts ran through my mind. We were in a gigantic amusement park and we were missing a beautiful little girl.

My cousin came up to me and told me to calm down. She said, "Let's go to the lost and found and if she is not there, *then* you get excited."

We found a police officer that took us to the lost and found and sure enough, there was Donya, sitting calmly at a table playing with some toys. The fact that she was so calm let me know that she had been there for a while and that she had probably gotten lost from Marie when they first walked away as opposed to when she was on her way back to the *"point."* I hurriedly gathered up the family and was anxious to get back to the house so that I could have a good stiff *drink* because my nerves were truly frazzled.

You can imagine my disappointment when Isidro said, "Ma, I got news for you. There will be no drinking. This is Virginia and the *ABC* stores close at 6 o'clock."

"What? You've got to be kidding." I didn't give a damn where we were, I needed a drink and I was going to have one.

During our travels the past couple of days, we passed a street, Avenue C, where I saw a lot of things being sold. And, being from New York, I was able to figure out very easily that if I went down to Avenue C, I would find what I wanted. We drove off of the interstate with my younger son Ricky jumping up and down in the back seat about how we were going to get robbed.

"Ricky," I said, "how is anyone going to rob two carloads of people? Just be quiet and sit down because you might not get robbed, but if you don't be quiet you are surely going to get a beating."

As we turned onto Avenue C, I saw a guy who had *the look* of someone who did nothing but knew everything. We pulled up beside him and I rolled down the rear window of the car and asked him to come over to the car. He came over and bent down to hear what I had to say. I asked him, "Where can I find the bootlegger?"

He said, "Me, Ma'am, I am the bootlegger. I sell Gin and Mist."

It wasn't until two years later that I discovered that Mist was Canadian Mist Whiskey. I told him that I would take the gin, but when he returned with a large opened bottle of Seagram's Gin and a dirty cup, I settled for a six-pack of Budweiser beer.

Isidro was shaking his head saying, "Only *my* mother could come all the way from New York to Virginia and find the bootlegger on her *first* try."

I happily took my beer back to the house, but after the first can, I fell asleep from exhaustion.

We spent the next few days going swimming, having picnics at Peanut's house, and just plain having fun. We only decided to head back to New York because our spur of the moment vacation days had run out. We came back to New York and settled into work and school, occasionally traveling to Virginia to visit for a day or two. My friend Myra had recently moved down there too, so it was like having a free vacation. No matter how many times I traveled to Virginia, the June trip always remained special to me. It was years later when I found out that it *too* was a gift from GOD.

The Few Good Years

Life was moving on rather uneventfully with everyone settling into their own routine. Sanyae was in college, Ricky was in grade school, Peanut was in the Navy and Isidro had opened up a car stereo shop in Virginia called Illusions. At that time in my life, I was really looking forward to Ricky growing up. And for the first time in my life, I could think about *me*. Little did I know that my life was going to change *and in a big way*, but not the way that I had been looking forward to for so much of my life.

CHAPTER SIX

THE ENEMY

Only a person who has had a loved one in prison or jail can know what it feels like. I will even go a step further to say that only a *mother* who has a child in prison can know the kind of pain that it brings. It is unlike having a child in the hospital where you can sit by their bedside, hold their hands, sponge their fevered head if necessary, and where you can have a say-so in what is being done to them. When your child goes to jail, all you can do is sit by hopelessly and wonder what is going to happen to them next. You have absolutely no input into anything that happens to them. You can't call them to see if they are alright. If things are not going the way you think they should, you have no one to call and complain to. You can yell and scream, you can cry your heart out, but the cold hard fact is that for the first time in your life you do not have one word to say in regards to what does or does not happen, where your child is concerned.

As a mother, it is next to the worst feeling in the world. Later on, I will tell you what the worst is. Like I said before, when my son was led from the courtroom with his hands cuffed behind his back, I felt like someone had plunged a knife into my chest. I could have died right there on the spot, but then I could not even do that because I could not help him then. I did not know what laid ahead for him. I thought of things like, *has he eaten? Did he get to bathe? Is he feeling okay?* And most of all I wondered if he was afraid. I know my son was not a sissy or anything, but I could not help thinking that he had to be afraid because he did not know what laid ahead of him. Once the feeling passed, I began to feel angry. I felt angry at everything and everybody that had a part in my son being where he was at that moment and, that included me. I kept wondering what went wrong and where it had gone wrong. Most of all I was angry at that punk bastard J.P. If that bitch had not been such a punk, he would not have been sitting in the witness protection program singing like a happy gay parakeet. My son did not know J.P. was a punk, but I surely did. I found this out when my friend Terry kicked his ass on 225 Street and Lanconia Avenue

As I stood outside of the doctor's office watching the fight, I could not help but think, *"Damn, if she didn't have on those high heeled shoes, she would probably kill that nigga."* I don't know what he did to her, but whatever it was, she was not having it and I was almost waiting for him to go get his brothers on her because even *he* had to know that his sisters did not stand a chance since *he* had gotten his ass kicked so badly.

My second run in with J.P. came a few years later when he came to my building with his crew looking for my neighbor's boyfriend. The poor girl came crying at my door saying that her boyfriend *Buzz* had owed J.P. fifteen dollars and that J had given him fifteen minutes to get the money or it would go up to a hundred dollars. I told Yvonne to go home and lock her door and not to open it and if things got bad, call the police. The next night, Mr. Big Bad J.P. came knocking at my door asking for Buzz. I told him in no uncertain terms that Buzz did not live there and not to knock on my door ever again. He attempted to intimidate me by punching one fist into the palm of his other hand, but I did not show him any fear and I simply took my dog Lucky and went downstairs, both to walk the dog *and* to get the piece of shit away from my door. I know he had a problem with people, especially women who did not show fear of him, and to this day I never knew if he was afraid of me *or* the dog.

How I wish I had been able to see the future because if I had, I would have put that maggot out of his misery that night and saved a lot of people a whole lot of misery, especially myself. As big and bad as J.P. was, he was not bad enough to save his mother from a bullet. I guess the saying, *"Live by the sword, die by the sword"* is true. Old Lady P caught a bullet one Friday afternoon during an escalating fight between her grandson and another neighborhood kid. I guess she didn't realize that everyone in the world was not afraid of the big bad P's even though they all had faces that would stop the local clocks, especially the mother.

The P brothers would beat up the young boys in the neighborhood if they didn't take the big, fat, ugly ass sister of theirs out. She was so damn fat, black and ugly, that some of the boys took the beating rather than take that *garbage truck* out.

I can remember the day that Old Lady P got shot like it was yesterday. It was a bright, sunny Friday afternoon. From what I heard, her grandson got into a fight with the next door neighbor's child. When he did not win the fight, his grandmother went inside and got a bigger grandson. The other little boy went inside and got his big brother. Grandma

P went back inside and got a *bigger* grandson and the little boy went and got a *bigger* brother. When it looked like the P's were losing the battle, Grandma went and got the biggest grandson in the house, and that is when things began to get ugly. The little boy ran to get his sister's boyfriend. Seeing that the odds were stacked against them, the P's retreated to the safety of their apartment. I guess the sister's boyfriend was upset about being dragged out of bed at 12 noon so he took out his frustrations on the P's door, meaning, he pulled out his gun and fired a shot at the door. What he did not know was that Grandma P was standing behind the door and caught a bullet in her stomach. I was relaxing at home when my phone rang. I picked it up and it was my friend *Frances* with the news. She said, "Mommy T, guess what happened?" Before I could even assume what was going on, Frances came out and told me. She blurted out, "Mrs. P got shot today. Just moments ago."

I said, "Really?" like if I were surprised.

"Yup, and she's on her way to the hospital now. They say she ain't gon' make it."

I could tell that Frances was probably on the other end of the phone examining her freshly painted fingernails or something because she was fly like that. Very calm like and almost speaking in a whisper, I asked, "How bad is it? Do you think she's going to make it?"

"I don't know, but I'ma call you back when I hear something, okay, sugah?"

"Mm hm," I mumbled.

"Bye, sweetie."

"Bye, bye." Frances and I hung up at the same time. But when my phone touched its base, a smile crept on my face. An old saying came to mind..."*What goes around, comes around.*" Before I could scold myself about feeling good about someone else's misfortune, the phone rang again. It was my friend Karen, from the projects.

"Teresa, you hear the news?" she asked excitedly.

"What news?" I was fronting like if I didn't already know.

"Old Lady P got killed."

"Well, how do you know that she's dead?" I wanted to know how she knew the well being of this lady when things had only recently popped off.

She answered by saying, "I heard everyone talking about it when I was taking my children to school."

I knew it was wrong, but I was feeling *real* good. I did not want to get too happy just yet though because I had to first make sure that she was dead for real. I thought about how she used her motherly touch to get my son to go to her house and be set up by the government. I had always blamed her more than I did her old broke down son. He was in jail, trying to get himself out, but she was a mother. How could she do this to someone else's child when she had so many children of her own?

The phone rang again and jolted me out of my thoughts. It was Frances with the news that Mrs. P was indeed *DEAD*. I jumped out of my chair and yelled, *"YES!"* I could not wait for my Isidro to call so that I could share the news with him.

I began walking up and down the house mumbling to myself that she got what her hand called for. She had destroyed my family and now her family was going to be destroyed too. It was such a good feeling that I did not know what to do. Isidro usually called on Fridays since he knew I was off from work. *Where was he now? When was he going to call?* I had not had this much good news for him in a long time. Then it hit me. This was wrong. I was not supposed to feel this good about anyone getting killed. I was supposed to forgive and place the situation in God's hands. Yeah, that was the way it was supposed to be, but that's not the way it was. Mrs. P had helped the Feds set my son up and now she had gotten killed and I was feeling *damn* good about it. In fact, I felt so good that I began to feel guilty and I got on my knees and asked God to forgive me for feeling so good about her getting killed. I stayed on my knees for quite a while, but when I got up, I was *still* feeling good, and I knew it was wrong. I just couldn't help it. I thought about J.P. and wondered if he had gotten the news as fast as I did. I could picture him being brought into a chaplain's office in some prison *snitch unit* and being told that his mother had passed away. I could imagine him asking what happened or asking to be allowed to call his family. I could just see his face upon learning that she had been shot. He would be filled with rage, but he would not be able to do anything about it. I just kept feeling better and better. I felt so good that I decided to go to the *projects* and see for myself if the news was really true. I showered and dressed in record time and then I hit the streets.

• • •

I walked up the block with more pep in my step than I'd had since my son had been arrested. I stopped at the corner deli and purchased a daily newspaper. The first thing I thought was that the next day the front page would have old lady P's picture with the headline, *"Grandma gets shot in NYC Housing "Projects"*. I smiled and continued on to the bus stop and waited for the bus to come. When the bus finally arrived, I boarded it and was glad to find it almost empty. I did not want people to be staring at me and wondering why I was smiling like the cat that swallowed the canary. I took a seat and read my newspaper while the bus rumbled on from stop to stop. I was so engrossed in the newspaper that I did not realize how far the bus had traveled. When I looked up, I was in front of my church. I pushed the strip and ran to get off the bus before it pulled off again. I had to go into the church to pray and ask God to please take these feelings away from me. I knew it was wrong, really wrong, to feel so good about someone dying and I needed to get into that church in a hurry and ask for God's help.

I went inside the sanctuary, and got down on my knees in front of Saint Jude, the patron saint of difficult cases. I knew it was going to be difficult to get rid of those feelings. I prayed so long that I lost track of time. When I finally did get up and go back out into the sunshine, I felt much better. I stood in front of the church and let the warm sun shine down on my face. I felt better about my feelings and I was filled with a sense of well being. I got on the next bus and continued on my way to the projects, still thinking of the P family. Even though I had just left the church asking God to forgive me for my evil thoughts, I could not help thinking that if you looked closely and long enough at their name that right smack dab in the middle would be the word *"rat."* *"God forgive me for these thoughts."*

I knew years earlier that that P person was going to cause a lot of grief and drama for a lot of mothers from the projects. I can even remember when he ran his Intercrime Gang. He had a following of a bunch of kids who were probably all scared of him. They would go through the projects terrorizing people, beating them up and taking their coats and sneakers. J.P. never actually did anything himself although he was the ringleader of the gang. He did all of the talking while the rest of the group did the actual robbing and beatings. I guess there were too many P kids to afford the latest fashions that the kids were wearing at the time, so he resorted to stealing in order to fit in with the crowd. He even had his own *court* in the community center for the kids who did not follow his rules. Imagine that...*using the community center that was paid for by tax dollars to terrorize the neighborhood children.*

I remember when my friend Joyce brought her son Steven to this court one day. I couldn't figure out why she went to court instead of going to the police department. She was probably smarter than I was and knew that the police weren't going to do anything because he probably had them afraid too. J.P.'s Intercrime days lasted until he was finally arrested by the Feds and carted off to jail where he belonged, *or so we thought.* He was really in the witness protection where he was probably being trained to become a professional snitch because as soon as he was released, he set up his so-called best friend *Danny.* It was not until years later that Danny would finally find out that J. was the one who had been setting him up for years. Danny is still in prison where he will most likely spend the rest of his life while the rat bastard J.P. is free to roam the world and wreak havoc on someone else's life.

CHAPTER SEVEN

THE PRISON YEARS

Having a loved one in prison can take a toll on the entire family emotionally, physically and financially. Throughout the seven years, seven months and one day that Isidro was in prison, our family met the most mean-spirited people on the planet. Only a person who has gone to visit someone in prison will know what I mean. Since most of the places that we had to visit were miles away, we usually hit the highway at midnight so that we could get there by eight in the morning for the visit. It took some time but after a while, I figured out what to do and what not to do when we went to visit. The first thing we needed was money. We would have to gas up the car and then get a couple of hours sleep before our long trek. We had to make sure that everyone had the proper clothing or they would not be allowed in. We also had to put our identification cards in one place so that we would not forget them and we had to make sure that we had enough quarters for the vending machines to last us throughout the visit. Being a smoker, I had to remember to bring an unopened pack of cigarettes in because they would not allow you to bring in an opened pack. A couple of times I forgot to bring an unopened pack, so I had to improvise. The visit would frazzle my nerves and there was no way that I was going to sit there for five hours with no cigarettes, so I just stashed enough in my bra to last throughout the visit.

I would wake up the small children shortly before midnight, wash them up and get them dressed. The very last thing we would do was make everyone go to the bathroom. Everyone was usually tired and went back to sleep before we crossed the George Washington Bridge. We always had snacks in the car in case anyone got hungry and we tried to keep the drinks at a minimum because stopping at a rest stop could slow us down for a half hour or more. Since we were leaving at midnight, I would always take the front passenger seat because I have night blindness and was not able to drive in the dark.

I remember one time when Sanyae insisted that I drive for a while. I told her that I did not think that it was a good idea because it was still dark. I asked her to just keep going until it became daylight, but she was not going for it and continued to insist that I drive for at least an hour or so. Against my better judgment, I got behind the wheel and started to drive. All was going well until the driver in front of me sped up and left me in total darkness. I had been following his taillights for miles. I immediately began to slow down and after a while I was gripping the steering wheel with both hands as if that was going to help me to see where I was going. I came to a place along the highway where there was construction going on and the road narrowed down to one lane. For a time there was no one out there on the road but me, but I could see a tractor trailer coming up in the rear view mirror. He got right behind me and started to blow his horn for me to pick up speed. His headlights were blinding me and I began to go even slower and I started to shout, "I can not see."

All of a sudden everyone in the car was awake and Ricky started to scream, "Don't put the brakes on!"

I said, "I have to because I can't see."

Sanyae, who was wide awake now, said to pull over and let her drive again.

I said, "How the hell can I pull over when there is only **one** lane?" We drove on like that for a couple of miles and the first chance that I got I pulled over. Sanyae jumped out of the back seat like her drawers were on fire and took the wheel. That was the very last time that anyone had asked me to drive at night, or anytime for that matter.

We finally made it to the institution in one piece and prepared for the most trying time of the trip. After having been turned away for one reason or another, you can never take anything for granted until you are actually in the visiting room *with* your loved one. You have to go into the waiting area and fill out a visiting form for all of the adults. Since there were usually more of us than they would allow in at a time, we would usually visit one of Isidro's friends so that we would all be allowed to see him.

After filling out the visiting forms, we would hand them to the duty officer after checking to see that every *t* was crossed and every *i* was dotted. We would then sit and wait for our names to be called. When they called you, they would ask for your ID card and then you had to wait again while they checked to see if you were on the visiting list. Once this was done, you had to go through the scanner to make sure you did not have any unauthorized items. After visiting a few times I learned to leave anything that was not necessary for the visit in the car. They provided lockers for the things that were not allowed inside the visiting room, but I did not trust their lockers and having to wait for a locker key would only slow you down further.

I always left my pocketbook in the car because I did not like them rifling through my personal stuff. If all went well up to this point, you then had to hold out your hand so that they could stamp it with some kind of invisible ink that only showed up under a black light. Once this was all done, we were hurdled like cattle through a room that had locked doors at both ends. Each person had to hold their hand under the light so that an officer in a control room could see the stamp. After inspecting everyone's hand, the officer in the control room would open the door and we were then led up a small hill to another building. In all my years of visiting the federal prison, I found that the rudest and meanest officers were always in the visiting area and were waiting to do anything that they could to keep you from visiting your loved one. Once you reached the visiting building, you had to again wait for someone inside to open the electronically controlled door. When you got inside, you had to give your name *and* the name of the inmate that you were visiting to the officer on duty and then sit and wait for your loved one to come out. I usually ran to the vending machines so that I could get enough food to last throughout the visit because the machines emptied out fast and there was no other way to feed your loved one *and* the children except from the vending machines. This is why it was so important to have enough change when you went in because there was no way to get change.

It was always with great joy and sadness that I ran to hug my son when he came through the visiting room doors. I could not hug him right away because I had to wait until he handed his inmate ID card to the visiting room officer. I was happy to see him with no bumps or bruises and sad that I had to see him under those circumstances. For a while we told the children that he was in school, but after a time, they grew up and realized the truth. We would sit down and talk about what was going on at home and in the old neighborhood. He asked about the people he left on the outside, some whom I thought should have kept in contact with my son and at least *wrote a letter or two* if not *send some much needed money to him*. The entire time that we were there, the visiting room officers took turns harassing the visitors *and* the inmates, especially the children. They did not seem to realize that small children did not know that they were in a prison with so many seemingly meaningless rules.

They were always complaining that people were *"too close"* or the kids had to go to the bathroom *too* many times or anything that they could harp on. They were not satisfied with telling the inmates what to do It seems as though they took great pleasure in bossing around the visitors too. We would sit there with Isidro and talk and talk until we did not have anything else to talk about, then we would just sit quietly holding hands. The guards did not want us to get too close. I guess they did not think that a mother wanted to hug her son, if only for a short while.

When it came close to the end of the visit, everyone would start watching the clock. There was an art to getting out of prison too. You wanted to leave a few minutes early so that your loved one would not get caught up in the *"traffic"* going back and missing his evening meal. The hardest part of the visit was always leaving. You never knew when you would get back to visit again because the institution was so far away, but you always promised to get back again very soon.

After kissing my son goodbye, I always looked straight ahead because if I looked back, he would have seen the tears rolling down my cheeks and to see me cry would have made his time harder to do. One day his daughter, Dee Dee, told the duty officer that she was not ready to leave. It was kind of funny at first because when he came around letting us know that visiting hours were almost up, Dee Dee popped up and said, "I ain't ready to go yet." She did not understand that she did not have a choice. It became sad when she asked my son to come home with us and he said that he could not. She then said, "Well, I guess I'm going to spend the night with you then." I noticed tears in a few people's eyes at that point. As hard as it was for Isidro and I, I am sure that it was a hundred times worse for his children. They never understood why their father was in prison and frankly, neither did I. It was also hard on his brother and sisters, his father, grandmother and his nieces. When he went to prison, he had six nieces. His four nephews were born after he was there so they never got to know the love of their very special uncle and he never had the pleasure of spending quality time with the four of them.

By the time we got to the parking lot, we were all crying, except for Ricky. I know that he was putting up a front for his mother and sisters, but I am also sure that he was crying inside. Leaving Isidro behind those walls was like being stabbed in the chest. It hurt and made it hard to breathe. I was usually halfway home before I was able to pull myself together. There was one thing that never changed throughout the years of my visits to my son and that was the fact that I always came home with a profound feeling of helplessness and hopelessness.

• • •

It was on trips to the prison that I learned how to travel on the road. Very quickly I learned what to do or what not to do on a long road trip. I learned what to take and what to leave home. I also learned who to bring and who to leave home with a promise that they would go the *next time*." It would sometimes become a mini family vacation when we went to see Isidro. Since the institutions were always very far away, we would get together and stay for the weekend. Keeping in mind that all of the Federal prisons were located in rural small towns across the country, you can imagine that it was not always easy for us to find lodging for the weekend. Most of the towns did not have a *Super 8* Motel, *Best Western* or *Days Inn* Motels. They had the mom and pop type of hotel/motels that you see in the old western movies and most were not prison family friendly and all were rather expensive when you considered what they had to offer.

One time we stayed in a four-story hotel, which was a big deal for *cow-town* Pennsylvania. Only three or four people could get onto the elevator at one time and it did not have automatic doors. The door had to be closed by someone on the *outside* of the elevator and inside you had to pull a gate closed and then pray for it to move up. The best part of this particular hotel was the bed. It was one of those beds with the iron head and footboards. If one person sat on it at a time, it became sort of like a seesaw. In order to keep the mattress in position, it took two people at a time to sit down, one on either side of the bed. When it was time to go to bed, I had to wait for Ricky to lie down at the exact time as I did. We counted *one, two, three* and then we both laid down at the same time. This way, one person did not land on the floor and the other one in the air. After a couple of hours of sleep, one person would have to alert the other that they were about to move. *God forbid that one suddenly had to go to the bathroom during the night and suddenly got up.*

Another time we had the whole family with us. There was Peanut and her four children, Ricky, Sanyae, myself and one of Peanut's friends from Boston. We did not know that there was a soccer tournament in town that weekend and there were no hotel rooms available *at all*. We were told that there was a single bedroom on the top floor and that they would bring in a cot for us. I guess they did not know or did not *care* how many of us there were. Imagine nine people in a single room.

When we traveled with the children, we always brought along a hot plate because food on the road *and* in the prison was very expensive. After visiting hours, we would go back to the hotel and make hot dogs and pork and beans for the kids. We added bread and juice to swell it up in their little stomachs and they were good to go for the night. We took turns sleeping on the floor *and* on the cot. Since Peanut was in the Navy and was used to traveling with the kids, she did not mind sleeping in a single bed with three kids. Ricky and Sanyae took the cot with the other kid, and Kim and I took what little space there was left on the floor. I actually wound up sleeping under the bed. I made friends with the man in the laundromat across the street from the hotel so that when the walls of the room started to close in on me, I had somewhere to go and someone to talk to. Like I said before, these trips were not easy but they brought us together and we were together to see Isidro. We never told him that some of the places were so scary that when we went in for the night we would lock the door, put a dresser against it and stay put for the night. He had enough problems and we made sure that nothing unexpected happened. Isidro once said that he was on pins and needles when we left because a lot of things happened to families on the way home from a visit. I never knew where we faced more danger, on the road *or* in some of those small town motels. We were just doing what we had to do. And it was all worth it because it is what kept Isidro going in prison.

When my son was arrested, I think I went into a denial stage. I lied to myself for two years and kept telling myself that some miracle was going to happen to make the whole thing go away. How wrong I was about that. I can't even remember exactly when reality finally set in, but when it did, things became very painful.

I spent every waking moment wondering what was happening to my son. When I went to the bathroom, I wondered if he was allowed to go when necessary or did he have to wait until someone told him it was okay. When I opened a door with a key, I would wonder when was the last time that my son held a key in his hands. When I woke up in the middle of the night to get a blanket because I had become cold, I would wonder if my son had enough blankets to keep him from being cold.

The hardest thing for me to do during that time was to eat. I have always been a good cook and my son enjoyed eating my food. I always wondered what kind of food did my son have to eat? I remember eating a salad at work one afternoon. In the middle of the lunch I picked up a piece of cucumber and held it in mid air. I thought to myself, *"When was the last time that my son had a cucumber?"* I dropped the cucumber back into the plate and burst into tears. Nobody around could figure out what in the world had happened, but they all figured that it had something to do with my son because they had become accustomed to my sudden outburst of tears. Life was hard for me and each day that my son spent behind bars made it harder.

At one time, I avoided the mailbox because it only meant *bills*. Now, I rushed home to get the mail in hopes of getting a letter from my son. I also limited the time of my telephone conversations. I did not want my telephone to be busy, just in case my son called. I would only have long conversations after midnight because I knew that he could not call then. I looked forward to hearing from him although most of the time I had no idea of how I was going to continue to pay for the long distance calls. I could never tell my son that he could not call so I just talked to him and worried about how I was going to pay for it later. At times I paid the phone bill before I paid rent because I thought that without a phone, my son could not reach me. I was in such a state of mind that it did not occur to me that if I did not have a roof over my head I would not have a place to put a phone, but I paid the phone bill first and worried about the rent afterwards.

With four kids to support, money had always been tight for me, but at that point, it was being stretched beyond its limits. I was always borrowing from *Peter* to pay *Paul*, but I always found whatever was necessary, to help my son. In addition to the added expense of going to see Isidro *and* the astronomical phone bills, I had to also find money to send to him from time to time. He always told me that he had the same needs in prison as he did on the outside. He needed money for clothes and sneakers. One might say that they are issued clothing, but the clothing that they are issued consists of an ill-fitting khaki suit and a pair of government shoes that may or may not fit. This clothing is only used in the visiting room, so Isidro still needed everyday clothing, which was mainly sweat pants, underwear, socks, boots for the winter months and sneakers. He also needed money to do his laundry and to buy things like soap, deodorant, a toothbrush, toothpaste and occasionally cologne to keep his spirits lifted. No matter how hard it was, I had to send my son money from time to time. It would have been much easier if I could have bought the things on the outside and sent them to him, but in Federal prison you are allowed to receive one thing, and that is a post office money order. It was by the grace of God that I made it through those years with some sort of sanity.

Another thing that happened to me was that I became suspicious of everyone and I did not trust anybody. I hated talking on the phone and would cut people who called, off, telling them that I would speak to them when I saw them. At one time, I was a friendly outgoing person who would speak to everyone. Now, I backed off of anyone who attempted to be friendly toward me. If a stranger looked at me and smiled, I would give a blank stare in return and my look said, *"Do not say anything to me."* I am still like that to this day. The people who I avoided most were those who had spent time in jail. I went around thinking that everyone was trying to set me up to get evidence against my son. My son went to prison in late 1990 and his death occurred in 1998, but still to this day, I second-guess everyone else. If someone asks me a question, I immediately ask why they are asking it. I do not talk to strangers, not even to give directions. If someone comes up to me to ask a question, the answer is always the same, *"I don't know"* and then I keep walking. I don't care if someone is just lost or trying to be friendly because that is what got my son in trouble in the first place, *trying to help.*

I guess on the outside I looked normal to people who didn't know me very well, but inside my life had changed. Everything was divided into two categories, **before** and **after!** All events either took place before Isidro was sent away or after. I could no longer listen to the radio without crying. Whenever I heard a song, I would wonder if Isidro had heard the song. It either came out before or after he went to prison. Some of the worse times were when I heard a song that Isidro liked. I would listen to a little part of the song and then have to turn it off because it made me cry. After a while, I just gave up listening to the radio altogether. *People* in general began to bother me. If a person was happy, I would think that it was unfair that they were so happy while my son was suffering in prison. If a person was sad or complaining, I would snap and tell them that they were fortunate that they had their freedom, unlike the thousands of drug war prisoners that have yet to be released.

One of the worse times for me was when I would see someone who had recently been released from prison or jail. I would wonder why this person was given a second chance and my son was not. I began to lecture everyone about how the system was just waiting to lock them up. I lived with the fear that someone was going to come along and lock my other son up. I was afraid for him to go out of the house, especially at night. I would let him invite his friends over in order to keep him at home. This was not easy because Ricky was a wanna-be D-Jay and his kind of music drove me up the wall, but it was easier than having to worry about him while he was out of the house. I hated when he went out with more than one friend because *in my mind* the cops would see *two* young men as friends but *three* young men walking together would be seen as a gang. It got so bad that I didn't even want Ricky to go to school because I just knew that something was going to happen that would land him in jail. In fact, at some point I even took him out of school and had him enroll in the *City-As* High School Program. By sending Ricky to school only one day a week, I figured that I had lowered his chances of going to jail. This was one decision that I made that turned out to be a blessing.

CHAPTER EIGHT

ISIDRO AND RICKY

Isidro was never a problem when he was growing up unless you count his love for fast things. I never had to go to school for him like I did for Ricky. Because Ricky was such a spoiled brat, I always thought I would have Isidro to keep him in line during his teenage years. I can even remember the day we brought Ricky home from the hospital. Ricky was born with an infection so he had to stay in the hospital until he was thirteen days old. It was a bright, sunny Sunday morning and we were all ready for the new baby. I guess Isidro must have been more excited than the rest of the children because he was the only one who got up early that morning to go with me to the hospital to get Ricky. We drove to *North Central Bronx* Hospital in our old red Chevy van with no seats in the back. When we got to the hospital, Isidro decided to sit in the van and listen to the radio while I went inside to get Ricky. I went in the hospital to get Ricky and came back to the van about twenty minutes later and found Isidro right where I had left him. This was a good thing because Isidro, like I said, loved fast things and the van, although old, had a very good engine. I was just happy that he had not taken it for a spin or two around the block. He opened the door and I handed Ricky to him to hold during the drive home. I can still remember his smile when he looked down into Ricky's little face. We pulled up in front of our building and after I parked, I told Isidro that I was coming around to the other side to get Ricky to carry him upstairs. He said, "No, Ma, let me carry him inside because I've been waiting for this day for fifteen years." He carried Ricky into the building like a proud father instead of an older brother. That day was the beginning of a special bond between the two brothers. Every time I look at Ricky now I wish that I could have seen them two together as grown men.

Isidro had a very infectious smile and when I think of him, it makes me smile too. He was handsome from day one and everyone thought so too, from old ladies to little girls. I can remember riding in the good old red van with him one sunny afternoon. We pulled up to a stoplight and there was a cute little girl riding in a car that pulled up next to us. She looked at Isidro and said, "Hi, what's your name?"

He said, "*Sidro*" which is what we called him. She didn't understand him and asked him again. He had to repeat it two more times before she got it right.

She looked at him and smiled and asked him, "Do you want to come and see me some time?" We both burst out laughing. Like I said, everyone liked Isidro and his beautiful smile.

Isidro was funny too and always made everyone laugh. I remember once when he came home with his school pictures. He was about eight years old then. I looked at the picture and made a comment about how nice the class picture looked, but I wondered aloud why the teacher had such a funny expression on *her* face. He said it was because she had made a fart when the photographer was snapping the picture. Isidro didn't even lose his sense of humor when he went to prison. I can remember asking him why he did not talk to his counselor when he had a problem. His reply was, "Ma, the man weighs three hundred and fifty pounds and wears polyester pants that stick up the crack of his fat ass. He doesn't care about his own body so what makes you think that he could care about me?" I guess he had a valid point there.

When Isidro first got arrested, Sanyae and I ran around like chickens without heads. We were both feeling bad because we did not have any money and we thought that having a good lawyer would help Isidro. We didn't know back then that even if we had been millionaires, we couldn't have gotten him out of prison. I do not know why we just simply didn't look at John Gotti who was arrested the day before Isidro. We went from one attorney's office to another thinking that we could find one that would hear the terrible story and defend Isidro for what we were able to scrape together. I remember one attorney, a former senator, asked for fifty thousand dollars to take Isidro's case. I looked at him and said, "Sir, if I had fifty thousand dollars, I would have been indicted too." I guess they thought that because it was a drug case, there had to be some money hidden somewhere, but that was not the case. Having a sister and a cousin who were attorneys, I used to have a lot of respect and admiration for lawyers. My sister and my cousin both worked hard and put themselves through law school and I looked up to them even though they were both younger than me. Now, I look at lawyers as leeches who feed off of the misery of other people. They take the suffering of others and use it for their own personal gains. In Isidro's case, the attorneys who were supposed to be there to help him were the ones who did him the most harm. The legal defenders that were assigned to Isidro's case can be best described as *"special ed."*

The young attorney from the Federal defender's office must have sold her soul to the devil to get Isidro to agree to a plea agreement. That was clearly not in his best interest. It is my firm belief that on earth we pay for the things that we do and it gives me great comfort to know that one day she is going to have to answer to God for what she did to my son in that courtroom. Originally, Isidro's case was assigned to another attorney, but when the lawyer left to teach at Fordham University, my son's case was handed to *Miss Carsons*. I was really sorry about Mr. Weinstein leaving because I had a lot of confidence in him and he seemed like a very straightforward person. *Ms. Carsons*, however, was another matter. My gut feeling told me not to trust her because she always seemed nervous and shifty eyed. From day one, I felt that she did not have Isidro's best interest in mind.

I remember her calling me on the phone on Thursday, September 12, 1991. I remember the date very well for two reasons. The first reason is because it was my daughter Sanyae's twenty-first birthday and the second is because it was the day that police officer *Hector Fontanez* was killed in the Bronx. Anyway, Ms. Carsons called me to tell me not to come to court on Monday, September 16, 1991, because Isidro would not be going to court. She went on to say that the government had planned on superceding his indictment and that she was surprised that they had not done it sooner. The following Sunday, I went to the Metropolitan Correctional Center in Manhattan and when I spoke to Isidro, he knew nothing about his court date being cancelled. I decided to go to court as scheduled and was not surprised to learn that the case was still on for that day. I was told that the time had been pushed back, but the case was still on. I went to the courtroom, which was still empty, probably because it was lunchtime, and took a seat. I began to pray to

God to please help my son. As soon as the door opened and Ms. Carsons walked in, I knew that there was something terribly wrong. Any other time that I saw Ms. Carsons she would greet me with a smile. This day her face registered shock. The look she gave me said that I was not supposed to be there. I was immediately angry because she had lied to me and told me that my son's court date had been postponed. Before I was able to approach her and ask her any questions, my son was led into the court handcuffed. A couple of Federal agents came in right behind Ms. Carsons. Isidro looked back at me with a blank stare before he was seated at the defense table. When the judge came in, the prosecutor told him that they had reached a plea agreement.

"What?" I uttered out loud which made everyone look in my direction.

Again, Ms. Carsons gave me that look that said that I was not supposed to be there.

When I heard the charges to which my son was pleading guilty, I jumped to my feet and said, "No, son." I was politely pushed down into my seat by a Federal agent, who leaned over and whispered for me to be quiet or that I would go to jail too. I was floored! The only reason I *did* sit down and remain quiet was because I had no doubt that they would lock me up, which did not scare me at all, but I knew that I could not help my son if I was in jail too. Why was my son pleading guilty when he had told me as recently as the day before that he was anxious to have his day in court? My head started spinning and it seemed that something very heavy had been placed on my chest making it hard to breathe. There were a few on and off the record conversations between Ms. Carsons and the prosecutor, and it was all over. Isidro had pleaded guilty. I wanted to die, I wanted to scream, but I just bolted from the courtroom where I met the prosecutor in the hallway. I looked her straight in the eye and said, "I hope you get cancer of the cervix." I don't know why I said that, but I guess it was the nastiest thing I could think of at the time.

When I got outside of the court building, the sun was blinding, but it was the tears that kept me from seeing. Again, I had that feeling of not being able to breathe. I hurried up and ran down into the subway to get the train that would take me back to the Bronx. I wanted to get as far away from that courthouse as I could. When I got on the train, I sat down and began looking in my pocketbook for something with which to clean my face. People on the train were staring at me, but I didn't care. All I cared about was my son and what had been done to him in that courtroom. I felt like the world was closing in on me. After riding a few stops I knew that I could not stay on that train. Inside I felt like I was falling into a bottomless pit and that underground train was not helping any. I got off at the next stop and fled to the street where I stood for a minute taking a couple of deep breaths. For a moment I felt better, but that sinking feeling came back again. So I flagged down a Yellow Cab that was coming in my direction. I don't think he had any intention of stopping for me, but he got caught by the red light and was unable to drive off before I got into the back of the car.

I jumped into the back seat before he had a chance to protest and when he did turn around to face me, the look on my face told him that I was not the one that day. After giving him directions to my house, I sat back and looked out of the window. All I could think of was how my world could be so dark on such a bright sunny day. When I got in the house, I closed all of the blinds, got into bed fully clothed and began to sob out loud. I don't know how long I stayed that way, but when I looked at the clock and saw that it was almost three in the afternoon, I knew that I had to pull myself together because Ricky was coming home from school soon and I did not want him to see me in that condition. *How could this be happening?* My grandfather served in World War I, my father served in World War II, my brother served in the Vietnam war, my daughter, Peanut, was presently in the US Navy, and Isidro himself had been in the Army, and this was how this country was going to pay us back. Something had to be done to help my son and I did not know what it was.

I don't know how long I walked around in the pain-induced fog, but the only comfort I could find was in my sleep. I had two kids at home that I had to support and a son who was in prison that needed a lawyer immediately. I was in denial about the charges that my son was facing until I spoke to a friend from my job.

He said, "Don't keep saying he didn't do this and he didn't do that. Let's say for the sake of argument that he did everything that they said he did, *now*, how can we help him?"

I finally realized that he was guilty until we proved him innocent *instead* of the opposite. I think that was the day that I began to face reality and stopped telling myself that it was a nightmare and that I was going to wake up and every-thing was going to be okay. I also faced the fact that I could not afford a paid attorney and would have to work with the one that I had. It was obvious from day one that the Federal defender was not going to do *too* much to help Isidro, so Sanyae and *I* did what we could to help his case.

We met with the lawyer and filled him in on a lot of background things that related to Isidro and his case. We gave him names of people who we thought were friends who would speak to the investigators and let them know what kind of person J.P. was. We figured that if they could impeach J.P.'s testimony, then maybe Isidro would have a chance. We wanted to establish the fact that J.P. was a bully with whom no one would willingly get involved. We read about the con-spiracy laws and found out that in order to have a conspir-acy, it had to be knowingly and willingly, and the fact that J.P.

ruled by fear should have been a plus for our case.

We did not find out until much later that there was nothing short of an act of God that was going to get my son out of this *"big mess."* Sanyae was in school and I was working, but we both found the time to go to the Federal court and make photocopies of the documents that were in Isidro's file. We would then make more copies at work and then send them to Isidro. It was in making copies one day that we discovered that there were some altered documents contained in his file. There was an arrest warrant that was dated 12/12/90, but upon closer inspection you could see that the document was clearly altered. When we looked closely, we could see that the original date was 12/13/91, but the 13 had been changed to a 12 and the 91 to 90. Upon further research, we learned that when there was no physical evidence or corroborating evidence, there had to be an arrest warrant issued before an arrest could be made. There was never an arrest warrant in the files until we began asking about one and then all of a sudden, a warrant appeared. It was then that I began to see that we were not dealing with the honest upright people that they wanted us to believe they were. After dealing with the US Attorney's office, the Bureau of Prisons and the Federal court, I have found that some of these people are worse than the people they lock up. I find that the inmates are more honest, straightforward and above board than all of the law enforcement personnel that I have *ever* come across.

CHAPTER NINE

When Isidro was first arrested, there was no one for me to turn to but at some point Isidro found out about FAMM (Families Against Mandatory Minimums) and it was very refreshing to have someone to talk to who understood what I was going through. The first thing they did for me was set up an interview with a local television station. The news reporter's name was *Manny Teodoro*. He was doing a story on Crack Cocaine and Mandatory Minimums and how it affected minority communities. I was so happy because I thought that finally something was being done. I was foolish enough to believe that as soon as the story got out, people were going to be enraged and do something about it immediately. Back then I did not know anything about the Rockefeller Drug Laws because if I had I would have known that nothing was going to happen soon, but at least I had hope and that was something that I had not had up to that point.

The second thing that FAMM did for me was to put me in touch with other families who had similar problems, thereby creating a support network of families. They also made it possible for me to go to the US Sentencing

Commission Hearings which were held at the Thurgood Marshall Building in Washington, DC. Had it not been for the love of my son, I know that this was something I would have never had the opportunity to experience.

As soon as I would return home from one of these events, I would rush and write Isidro a long letter detailing the events of the day to him. He would also call on the phone and I would tell him almost the same things that I had written in the letter. The letters were usually more accurate because I could relate the events without being interrupted. We would talk about what happened and what did not happen and we would make an outline for the next event so that we could cover anything that we may have left out. Isidro once told me that he hardly went to the gym because he spent most of his time in the law library researching the laws that had put him where he was and I felt that if he worked on the inside and I worked on the outside, *together*, one day, we would make a difference.

After joining FAMM, I learned of several other groups that were fighting for reform of the harsh mandatory minimum sentencing laws and I joined several of them. I joined the *November Coalition* and the *William Moses Kunstler Fund for Racial Justice*. On May 8, 1998, I joined a group of people for our *first* rally, who would later become *Mother Of The NY Disappeared* which took place in front of Rockefeller Center. Ten days later I would find out that on that very day, my son had fallen out unconscious on a prison bathroom floor, but on that day *I* was full of energy and hope.

I was especially happy that day because I had heard from my son who had stopped calling as frequently as he always had and this had me a little worried, but I happily informed him that I was on my way to a rally on his behalf and I was hoping that he would feel as good about this as I was feeling. I was at first a little apprehensive because I did not know any of the other people there, but after a few minutes I just joined the action. We all had posters of our loved ones who were in prison and we were passing out leaflets about the Rockefeller Drug Laws. At first, Ricky did not want to pass out leaflets, but soon he was caught up in the frenzy of things and he was having a good time. In fact, he was having such a good time that when a city bus would pull up, he would jump on the bus and pass out a few leaflets and then jump back off. We were only there for a couple of hours, but that day was *so* meaningful because on *that* day I met some friends who gave me what I needed most at the time, and that was hope. I felt that finally things were starting to happen and I was a part of it.

At the end of the rally we exchanged phone numbers and planned to meet there again the following week. While I was out there passing out leaflets, I met some interesting people. One of them was *Regina Stevens*. Her son, *Terrence Stevens*, was serving time in a state prison for drugs. What made his case so special is that Terrence has a form of muscular dystrophy, which has left him paralyzed almost from the neck down. He is totally dependent and is confined to a wheelchair. At night when Terrence is sleeping, he has to be turned every two hours so that he can continue to breathe. I remember thinking at the time that I don't know how I could handle it if Isidro was incapacitated and incarcerated too. Regina was a strong woman and I know I could never have imagined myself in her place. Regina was out there with her poster too and we were both trying to make something happen to bring our sons home. Some people passing by stopped to look at our posters and to express concern about the plight of our loved ones, but others passed by seeming totally indifferent, hardly glancing at the posters. Some people were very opinionated and told us out right, *"Don't do the crime if you can't do the time."* We were not deterred however, and we just kept on passing out leaflets and collecting signatures for our *drop the rock* campaign. Since that day, Regina and I have done a lot of work together to change the laws that were locking up our young sons for the best years of their lives.

CHAPTER TEN

While my son was in prison, I had to try hard to make a normal life for those that he left behind. During the day, no matter what I was doing, my mind always wandered back to Isidro. At these times I would try to think about the good times and concentrate on something that made me happy so that I would not burst out in tears at my desk. I used to reach back into time and think of the happy carefree days when my children were young, and the biggest problem I had was how to get everyone's homework done and get the kids to bed on time. The worse time for homework was when the school year was coming to a close. When the weather was warm, everyone wanted to be outside. One of the best ways to do this was to promise them that if they did the right thing all week, we would go on a trip when the weekend came. Of course, one of their favorite places during the warmer months was an amusement park or a carnival.

I remember one weekend in June when Hector and I decided that the kids had been good all week and that they deserved an outing. We decided to go to Coney Island in Brooklyn, New York. We arrived at the amusement park on a bright sunny Sunday afternoon. We strolled around the park eating Nathan's hot dogs and cotton candy and drinking sodas. After the food it was ride and game time. We all played a few games, won a few prizes and then went to the go-carts. After a couple more rides, Isidro and Peanut decided that they wanted to go into the Spook House. I immediately let them know that they would have to go in alone if they really wanted to go in because I had no intention of going in and I admitted that I was afraid to go in. They were real brave and agreed to go in alone. The last thing that I said to them was, "Keep your hands and feet in the car and do not get out of the car until you get back outside." Hector, Sanyae and I waited patiently outside as Isidro and Peanut went in for the scary ride. A few minutes later, the car came out with Isidro sitting there with his hands covering his face and his eyes squeezed shut. I yelled, "Where is Peanut?"

He opened his eyes, looked around and said, "I don't know."

I started screaming, "Oh, my God, Oh, my God."

The man running the ride said, "What happened?"

I said frantically, "My daughter is still in there somewhere."

The ride operator looked over at the guy working with him and said, "Shut off the juice. There's a kid inside."

The way he said it made me realize that something terrible could happen inside. It only took them a few minutes to find Peanut, but in that short time, I died a thousand times. "That's it," I said, "time to go." Of course everyone was mad at us because no one was ready to leave, but as far as I was concerned, the party was over. Everyone went home with a long face, but come to think about it, every other time that we went to a carnival or amusement park, they came home with the same face. No matter how long you stay or how much money you spend, the kids are never happy when it is time to go home. This is just one of the many places my mind wandered when I was thinking of my son Isidro. Bright sunny days always remind me of Isidro.

CHAPTER ELEVEN

No matter how bright and sunny my days were, my nights were full of pain. When the lights were turned off and all was quiet, my mind quickly drifted to my son. I would go over and over in my head about what I did or did not do. I would ask myself *what went wrong* and *what could I now do?* I would sob quietly so that no one would hear me. I would look up at the ceiling while the tears rolled silently down my cheeks. This is exactly what I was doing on the night of May 18, 1998.

I had left work early so that I could go home and get some sleep because I had an early class the next morning. I went home and took two *Tylenol PMs* and went to bed. I don't know how much time had passed when the telephone rang. I started not to answer it thinking that no one knew I was home and that the call was probably for Ricky. After the fourth or fifth ring, I decided to pick it up. The caller was a female with a heavy voice that said, "I know you don't know me, but I am calling on behalf of your son, Isidro. Like a week and a half ago, Isidro passed out in the prison bathroom and he was never given adequate medical attention. I also heard that he'd been acting strange lately." Then she asked me, "Do y'all have a history of any mental illness in y'all's family?"

I placed my hand on my chest because I was shocked at what I was hearing. Then I kindly said, "No, and are you sure about what you're telling me?"

"Mm, hm," she mumbled. Then she said, "I was told that you should call the prison and tell them that the *big shots* heard about what went on and are coming out there to investigate." She paused for a moment as if she was checking her mental notes to see if she left anything out, then she said, "Oh, yeah, when I hear something else, I'll holla at you."

Something deep down inside of me told me that this call was real and that my son's life was in danger. It is something that only a mother *knows* and *feels*. Even though my son was far away and had been for some time, I was still connected to him in a way that no distance could destroy. I started to get that tightening feeling in my chest that I always got when something was going on with one of my children. I jumped up and put my clothes back on and headed out of the door. I had disconnected my long distance service several years before because I did not need the extra charges on my phone bill and I felt that if people far away wanted or needed to talk to me that they would have to call *me*. The extra money could go into Isidro's account so that *he* could call home. Because I had no long distance service, I ran four blocks away to the twenty-four hour store and bought four $10 calling cards. I needed to get in touch with the Bureau of Prisons as soon as possible. I ran back home and grabbed the phone and began dialing the *FCI Allenwood* in *White Deer, Pennsylvania*. The officer on duty asked if I was calling for an inmate or staff and then asked for my son's name and registry number. I asked him, "May I speak to someone on staff that could give me information regarding the health and well being of my son?"

He put me on hold for a few seconds and then came back on the phone and said, "Mrs. Aviles, your son is fine."

I asked him, "How could you find out in such a short period of time how *one* inmate was fine when there are over fourteen hundred inmates in your institution?"

I then asked, "May I speak to your highest ranking official on duty?" I was again put on hold and then I spoke to another official who told me the same thing, that my son was "fine."

For months I had been noticing a change in my son that I really didn't like. I did not like the fact that he was losing weight and that his complexion was always pale and ashy looking. I also did not like the fact that whenever I tried to speak to someone at the institution about this, I was given the brush off. My son said he did not like eating the food because other inmates *"Did things to the food."* I had previously called his counselor, Mr. William Campbell, and told him that I did not like the way my son looked. I also told him that I did not want my son to know that I had called because I did not want him to think that I was checking up on him like he was a child.

As soon as I reached home that evening, Isidro was on the phone asking why I had called up to the prison *"all hysterical"* checking up on him. I was so angry that Mr. Campbell had gone behind my back and had done the very thing that I had specifically asked him *not* to do and that was to tell my son that I had called.

When I received the call from this unidentified woman, I knew that my fears were founded and that there was something wrong with my son. Knowing full well that I was only going to get the brush off on the phone, I decided to travel to Pennsylvania to see how my son really was. I called both of my daughters and told them about the phone call. Peanut, who was in Boston wanted to know more and asked for the lady's phone number. I told her that this was not possible since the lady told me that she would call me back and that I would have to wait for her call. Sanyae decided to take the day off from work and go to Pennsylvania with me. Ricky also decided to take the day off from school and go along. We didn't have a car at the time so Sonja, my granddaughter, Laquisha's mother, volunteered to lend us *her* car and to also go along with us. Sanyae's friend, Jenny, also offered us the use of her car so we did not have to worry about how we were going to get there.

I don't know what anyone else did, but I spent the night pacing the floor and smoking cigarette after cigarette. About four o'clock in the morning, I ran out of cigarettes and that is when I really began pacing up and down. It's funny how I was afraid to go outside for a pack of cigarettes, but I had not been afraid to go blocks away when I needed the phone cards to check on my son. I tried lying down a couple of times, but that did not work either. I searched the ashtrays again for a butt *big* enough to get a couple of puffs off of, but there were none. In the back of my mind I kept thinking *there is something wrong with my child. He needs me and I am nowhere around.* It was a terrible feeling. Every time I took a deep breath I would get a sinking feeling in the pit of my stomach.

Finally it was 5:30 a.m. and I knew that the corner deli opened up about that time. I went out and got two packs of Marlboro Lights, a cup of coffee and the Daily News. I must have had some look on my face because one of the deli owners commented on how terrible I looked and asked me if there was anything he could do to help. I mumbled something about my son being sick and me not being able to get to him. I had forgotten the fact that he had never met Isidro and he thought I was talking about Ricky. I told him that Ricky was fine, but my *older* son needed me and that it would take me hours to get to him. He said that he would pray for my son and for us to get there and back safely. His words were very comforting to me and I told him thank you. At the time, I did not know that the young man was battling cancer, but when I found out later, I remember thinking how special it was for him to put aside his *own* concerns and offer us his prayers.

Daylight finally came and with it the realization that there was nothing that I could do for my son from the outside of the institution. I had to get inside and find out what was going on and take it from there. Sanyae must have heard the urgency in my voice because she was there bright and early as was Sonja. She came in a car with a broken windshield and we decided that we had enough problems and we did not need any further drama by getting stopped on the interstate with a cracked windshield so we decided not to use her car. Jenny said that we could take *her* car, but we knew that it was not likely that we would arrive back by the time she got off from work. She lived upstate and had no other way of getting home. I called my friend Myra and she said not to worry, just come and get her car and she would find a way home.

After asking a few questions, she said, "Just come and get the car and go see about your son."

Ricky, Sanyae and Sonja went to get her car and came back right away. Even though it was beautiful outside, I knew that the day did not hold a lot of promise, I could feel it in my bones. My suspicions were reinforced when the three of them came back and said that they almost had a serious car accident. I felt like a black cloud was looming over my head. Because everyone was so nervous and upset that I did not think it was a good idea for *any* of us to drive, I decided to go and get my friend Paul and asked him to drive us. He didn't want to at first, but then he *too* heard the urgency in my voice *and* saw the pain in my face. After that he changed his mind. I had also voiced my concerns about Isidro's well being to him several times over the past few months. So we all set out and headed to White Deer, Pennsylvania, where we did not know what we were going to find.

The ride there was uneventful and everyone in the car was unusually quiet. Even Ricky, who normally blasted the radio everywhere we went, was quiet and cooperative. We arrived at the Low Security Correctional Institute about two-and-a-half hours later. My feet felt like they were lined with lead when I stepped out of the car. As we opened the door to enter the lobby, there was a group of people all in business attire leaving the prison. I remembered what the anonymous caller had said on the phone the night before, *"Call the prison tomorrow because the big shots will be there."* I couldn't help but think that these people had to be the *big shots* that she was speaking about. From the looks on their faces, they knew who *we* were too! They were discussing something and I immediately knew that they were discussing my son, and whatever they had seen or heard, they were not happy about. There was no way they could get around us and when we asked if they were there about inmate *Isidro Aviles*, they *did* stop. In what could best be described as a *"drive-by meeting,"* we were again told that Isidro was fine. We were also told that he was going to be taken to a local hospital for testing. Of course the first question we all had was *why was he being taken to a hospital if he was fine* and the second was *could we see him to see for ourselves if he was, in fact, fine as they put it.* We were told that we could not see him because it was not his regular visiting day, and to this very day I wonder what would have happened if it *had* been his visiting day.

One of the people in the group that did not work for the prison stopped to speak to us. She told us that she had spoken to Isidro a couple of weeks ago at my request and at the time he *did* seem fine. She also went on to tell us that she had seen him that morning and that she had several concerns. She went on to demonstrate to us how Isidro was walking when she saw him and what she did brought me to my knees. For her to describe my young healthy son as walking like a ninety-year-old man made me scream out in anger and pain. *What happened to my son? Why had he not been taken to the hospital on the day that he passed out? Why were other inmates caring for him instead of trained medical staff?* And, most of all, *why did we have to get this information from an anonymous caller instead of from an official at the Bureau of Prisons?* We knew that we were being lied to. This person did not call us to alarm us for nothing. She called because she was a caring, concerned individual and the Bureau of Prisons was more interested in how we got the information instead of the condition of my son. They told me that inmates were not supposed to call other inmates' families with information and when I said it could not have been an inmate who called because it was a female, the shock registered on their faces. *What was going on behind those walls that they did not want our family to know?*

CHAPTER TWELVE

I used to sit and wonder if the people I had been dealing with the past seven years had families. It was hard for me to imagine someone doing such evil things during the day and then going home to their husbands, wives and children at the *end* of the day. Up to this point in my life, I was not aware that evilness was something that could be turned on and off. I had been under the impression that it was something that one was born with and that stayed with the person their entire life. I could not understand why these people did not understand the fact that Isidro had a family and that his family loved him and wanted to help him in *any way* that we could. When we returned home from the Low Security Correctional Institute in White Deer, Pennsylvania, we all began to write letters and make telephone calls on Isidro's behalf. I took off from my job and then sat down at the kitchen table and began to handwrite letters to everyone and anyone who I thought could or *would* help us. I wrote to the *Montel Williams Show*, the *Oprah Winfrey Show*, the *Jenny Jones Show*, the *Ricky Lake Show*, and several other television stations. I also wrote to *President Clinton* and several congressmen and senators. I never received an answer from the television shows, but I did get a call from the *White House*. The caller said that I had put my phone number on the letter, but I had forgotten to put my address on it. I could not imagine that the *White House* staff was not able to find a woman from *the Bronx* without having an address. Boy, we are really in trouble. I really can't figure out why they wanted my address because once I gave it to them, I never heard from them again.

Ricky went to school and was able to get one of his guidance counselors to write some letters for his brother. It was ironic that this same counselor was very familiar with *Ina Carsons*, the attorney that was supposed to be there to help, but actually caused my son the most harm. Sanyae and Peanut also wrote letters on his behalf. One of Sanyae's professors at school wrote a very nice letter. Peanut also wrote a letter that was so powerful, I suspect that it was what made the officials break down and give us the visit that turned out to be our goodbye to our son. When I finished writing the letters, I took them down to the pharmacy a couple of blocks away and began to send them to everyone by fax. I was hoping and praying that someone would read my fax and respond to my plea for help.

From the day my son was arrested I wanted him to know that he was loved and that I was there to help him in any way that I could. Once he saw that he was not going to get any competent legal assistance without any money, he started working on his case himself. He would get documents and send them to me so that I could make copies for him. He also sent me to the Federal courthouse several times to get different documents that he needed for his case. In the beginning, I was real leery about going into the Federal courthouse, but after a while, I became a pro at it and was able to maneuver my way around fairly easily.

I remember once, Isidro had a legal brief to file and he needed several copies of the brief because he had to give a copy to everyone involved in the case. I had to get copies made at a printer and then I had to have the copies collated and legally bound. I had no problem getting the brief copied and collated, but I knew nothing about binding. When Isidro called, he told me of a place in New Jersey that would do it for me. I only had a little bit of money so I had to wait until I got paid before I could get this done, but the briefs had to be filed in court no later than three o'clock the next afternoon. I took the day off from work and then borrowed my cousin's van so that I could get out to Fort Lee, New Jersey, and then get back downtown to Federal court by three p.m. It was raining cats and dogs and the roads were very slick, but I made it to New Jersey without a hitch, but when I got there, the owner of the printing shop told me that it was too late for him to finish the work that day. I was so overwhelmed that I took a seat and began to sob. I had tried so hard to get this done for my son and at the last minute, things went wrong. Some people tell me that I am a professional crier meaning that when I cry, I cry so hard that it seems like I was getting paid to cry. You know, one of those people whose nose starts to run and their chest goes up and down and you just want to do anything to make them stop crying? Well, that's me when I cry and I guess it worked because I started to cry and say that I had to have this done for my son. I told him how my son and I had worked so hard to get it done and how it had to be in the court before three o'clock that afternoon and it was noon then. Before long, the owner of the shop went back into the pressroom and told his employees to stop what they were doing and to get the binding done for me.

I couldn't believe my ears. He said, "Stop the presses and get this done for this lady."

I looked up and said, "Thank you, Jesus."

While they were doing the binding, I kept offering the

man, *Mr. St. Louis,* money, but he steadfastly refused to take any. When the binding was done, the employees boxed them up for me and they *too* refused to even accept a tip. It was truly the work of God. Paul and I got back into the van and headed back towards Manhattan. We made it to the court-house and in our haste to get the brief to the judge, we got into the wrong elevator. Once we were on our way upstairs, we realized that we were in the elevator reserved for judges only, but by then, it was too late. When we got off the ele-vator, there was an agent sitting down reading a newspaper. He never even glanced our way. *So much for Federal court secu-rity!* We entered the judge's chambers and handed the brief to the judge's law clerk and I let out a big sigh of relief. We left the courtroom and started for home. I was full of mixed emotions. I was thinking that I should never have had to go through this, but at the same time, I was elated that I had accomplished something that was important to my son. I had a heavy load off of my mind. I sat down in the van, put my head back against the headrest and said, "I need a drink."

CHAPTER THIRTEEN

After my son went to prison, I was unable to sleep at night. I would lie in bed and a thousand thoughts would go through my head. They were always before and after thoughts. I would lie there and think of all of the good times we had together and I would plan for the party that I was going to give Isidro when he got out. After I received the anonymous call, all I could think of was Isidro just being alive. At first I would ask God to please let my son make a full recovery and then I would say, *"God, just let my son live, I will take him any way I can, but please, just spare his life."* Most of the time I would say, *"God, please don't take my child, if you have to take someone, please take me, but God, please don't take my child away from me."* I used to wonder why Isidro had to suffer so much. I said, *"If he was going to die, why did God let him linger in prison for seven-and-a-half years first?"* I wondered if God was thinking about me because I knew if Isidro had been taken away from me suddenly, I would have surely died, so I guess God's way of preparing me was by taking him away first. After these thoughts would pass, I would say, *"No, Isidro is not going to die. He is a strong person and he is going to make it through this too."* I would then ask myself if he was tired and was giving up.

I thought of something he always said to me when I scolded him about driving fast or riding recklessly on his motorcycle. He always gave me the same answer which was, "Ma, don't worry about me, I know I am going to die young and I am not afraid of dying!"

Now that I think back about it, he said that to me on several occasions and my answer was always the same to him..."Boy, don't talk like that."

The thought of him dying was too much for me to bear. One of those nights that I was unable to sleep I thought about Isidro suffering in prison. I was thinking that it would be too much for him to be disabled and *in* jail too. He was always so strong and independent. I could not imagine him having to wait for other people to take care of him. I started to ask myself, *What if he did not get better and had to be in prison sick and at the mercy of the other inmates and corrections officers* who I knew for a fact could be very mean. I decided to go to the *Grotto* and pray over it. I knew that in the end it would not be what I wanted, but what God wanted and even though it did not seem like it at the time, I knew that God knew best. I finally fell asleep like I had done many nights over the past few years, praying for my precious son.

When I woke up the next morning, I had my day planned out. I would go to the Grotto to pray and light some candles and then I would come home and continue my letter writing. It had been three days and I still had not heard from anyone. I took a cab to the Grotto because I was in a hurry to get there. Since the day was nice, I decided to sit outside. Because it was a weekday, it was very quiet and peaceful. I bought several candles and took them outside where I lit them and placed them next to the statue of *Our Lady of Lourdes*. I then sat down and began to pray. I asked both God *and* the Virgin Mary to please send some divine intervention to me. I asked them to please let my letters get into the hands of someone who would be willing to help me. I sat there for a long time enjoying the peace and tranquility. Ever since I was a young child I always had a sixth sense and on this day, I was thinking that I should enjoy the peace because it would probably be one of the last peaceful days that I would have for a long time. When I finally left, I decided to walk home because it was such a nice day and I could take my time and figure out what my next step would be. When I got home, I immediately lit the candle that I had bought at the Grotto and placed it on the refrigerator in front of a statue of the Virgin Mary that I kept there. I then went to check my messages and was surprised to find a message from Congressman *Thomas Manton's* office. I was so nervous and excited that I could hardly dial the phone and had to redial the number three times before I finally got it right. I spoke to a young man named *Ivan Larios* who said that the office had received my fax. He was very patient and listened to my story and then told me he would make some calls and get back to me. I didn't have much faith in him getting back to me because I had heard that line numerous times over the past several years, but I told him that I would be in the house waiting for both his call and possibly a call from the Bureau of Prisons. Mr. Larios did call back and told me he would be working with me and then asked several more questions. Over the next couple of weeks Ivan and I had several conversations and after a time, it appeared that he became as frustrated as I was because of the treatment we were getting from the Bureau of Prisons. I have to give it to Ivan though because he has the patience of *Job* because I am sure that it was not easy for him dealing with me, my family members *and* the Bureau of Prisons too. I guess it was at the point that he finally became fed up when we were unable to make some headway and find out where my son was.

CHAPTER FOURTEEN

In the midst of everything that was going on, my Aunt Eloise passed away in Philadelphia. When it rains, it pours and it was really storming in my life. We had just gone to Philly several months prior for the funeral of my father's brother, Uncle Herbie, and now we were back again for his wife's funeral. It seems that when a lot of bad stuff is happening at one time, you become numbed by pain and this was one of those times. I was just going through the motions by putting one foot down in front of the other to keep on keeping on. I was in church, hardly listening to the sermon but looking at my young cousins, Michael and Yolanda, and thinking how strong they were and how well they were holding up. They had just buried their father and now they were burying their mother, but they both seemed to be holding up pretty well. An unwanted thought crept into my head about how I would hold up under the same circumstances, and then all of a sudden a white dove flew into the church and over the casket where my Aunt Eloise lay in an apparently peaceful state. I guess she was so peaceful because she was going on to be with her beloved Herbert. For some unknown reason, when that dove flew in, I knew that before long I was going to have to bury my precious son. I burst out in tears and everyone thought that I was crying for Aunt Eloise, but it was Isidro I was crying for. As soon as the funeral was over and everyone went back to the house, I began making phone calls again. Since we were in the state of Pennsylvania, I thought that I could get some help from the officials there. It may have been my agitated state of mind due to all that I had been through, but I found the elected officials in Pennsylvania to be just as rude and obnoxious as the people at the Bureau of Prisons. I finally gave up and decided to wait until I got back to New York to speak to Ivan Larios.

We were all sitting around the living room talking about Aunt Eloise and the things she used to do and say. The atmosphere was very cheerful because Aunt Eloise was a funny lady who could make you laugh until you cried, and instead of sitting around being sad, we were laughing like crazy about some of the things Aunt Eloise did over the years. I don't remember who it was, but someone brought up the fact that Aunt Eloise had to have her cigarettes *and* had to play her numbers *every day*. I asked what her main number was and someone, probably Michael, said *"451."* I put back on my tight church shoes and headed up the block to the check cashing place so that I could play the number. I played the numbers and went back to the house and we all continued eating, drinking, talking and laughing. About an hour later, the daily number flashed across the television screen *451*. I jumped up and down and said, *"Yes!"* and *"Thank you, Aunt Eloise."* By then it was too late to go back down the street and collect the winnings and we had to head back to New York City. I would not be able to get back to Philadelphia until the following Friday, so I decided to wait until then to go back and collect the money. I was in Philadelphia collecting my lottery winnings, which was why I was *not* home when *the call* came in.

CHAPTER FIFTEEN

Wh_en I got back to New York City, I decided that I would have to go back to work because I had run out of vacation time and not knowing what was going to happen, I thought it best for me to get back to work. During the day I was on the phone constantly with both Peanut *and* Ivan Larios who were both trying to help me find out where Isidro was and what his medical condition was. It was at this time that we found out that Ricky had a hernia and would need surgery immediately. Although I had just gone back to work, I had to take off another day so that I could take Ricky to the hospital to have his surgery. It was just one thing after another and through it all, I could only think of Isidro, who was miles away and who I *knew* needed me most of all.

It was a bright sunny Friday morning when I took Ricky to *Our Lady of Mercy Medical Center Ambulatory Surgery Unit.* He would have the surgery and go home after he woke up from the anesthesia. I guess Ricky was nervous because he was blabbing on a mile a minute, which was not unusual for Ricky, but *this* morning he was jumping from one subject to another. I knew that the one thing that would take his mind off the surgery was money, so I decided to ask him did he fill out his disability form. My little trick worked because he began to figure out how much money his check was going to be. There were other people in the waiting room and they were amazed that all he could think of at the time was how much his check was going to be, but knowing Ricky, I knew that money was the one thing that was going to take his mind off of whatever else he may have been thinking of at the time. It's funny but when he *did* receive the check about six weeks later, he received the exact amount, to the penny, that he had figured out. Ever since Ricky was a little boy, he had been very precise where money was concerned, and the fact that he was about to undergo surgery did not change anything. Money was his number one priority.

As soon as they wheeled Ricky into the operating room I left the hospital. I couldn't wait to get to a phone so that I could call again and try to find out how Isidro was. Instead of going home, I went to my friend Paul's house which was only a few blocks from the hospital. This time I struck oil! I was able to speak to a doctor for the first time since Isidro had become ill. After holding on for several minutes, I was connected to *Dr. Shim.* He said that Isidro had been taken to a hospital and had recognized him when he saw him earlier that morning. I found it strange that he mentioned Isidro recognizing him when just days earlier I had been told that Isidro was *"fine."* He went on to say that Isidro was sick but that with medication he would get well soon. He mentioned Lyme disease and muttered something about Isidro having a tattoo. He seemed to be tap dancing around my questions so I just came right out and asked him, *"Is my son going to die?"*

He chuckled and said, "No, not now anyway." He then went on to tell me how long he had been a doctor and how many grandchildren he had. I can remember wondering why he was telling me all of this when the only thing I wanted to know was how my son was and when I could see him. I don't know if he thought I was impressed by the longevity of his career or the fact that he had so many grandchildren, but all I got from his conversation was the fact that he was an old man that should have *been* retired. I did not feel like the conversation was going anywhere and I was becoming very frustrated, so I told him that I would call him the following day to check on my son's progress. What I really wanted to do was get him off the phone so that I could run back to the hospital and check on Ricky. It's funny that even though Ricky had chronic asthma and I knew that anesthesia was dangerous for him, I was not worried about him. My gut feelings told me that it was Isidro who needed me the most that day. My heart was broken because I knew that my son needed me there to comfort and reassure him and I was no where around because the *Bureau of Prisons* would not allow me to be there for my child when he needed me the most. It was a very painful feeling, one that has not gone away with the passage of time. I picked up Ricky from the hospital, brought him home and put him to bed. I was wishing all of the time that I could have brought Isidro home too and gave him the love and care that I knew he needed. I spent the entire weekend catering to Ricky, bringing him food, helping him to the bathroom and back to bed, and all the time I kept hearing the words that the anonymous caller said. When she was describing Isidro's condition to me, she said, *"Your son can't even get to the bathroom on his own and the other prisoners are taking care of him, not the staff."* The whole time I was taking care of Ricky I was wishing with all of my heart that I could have helped Isidro in and out of the bathroom and make sure he was well fed and comfortable. The one feeling that no mother should have to have is the one of knowing that her child is sick and helpless and that she is nowhere around. This feeling has left a bitter taste in my mouth that just won't go away.

CHAPTER SIXTEEN

My calls to Congressman Manton's office became more frequent and more desperate. I was begging to see my son. I wanted to hold him in my arms and comfort him. I wanted to speak to a real doctor and find out what was going on with him. I wanted to know why I could not see him. He had been allowed visits before he became ill and I could not understand why I was not allowed to see him now. I kept asking myself what his condition *really was. How did he look? Had he injured himself when he fell out in the shower?* I had a million questions to ask about my son and no one to ask. After a time I began to feel angry, very angry. I would call the prison and usually be put on hold for long periods of time only to be disconnected, and when I called back I would get a busy signal.

I would call and ask to speak to Dr. Shim and would be transferred to five or six different extensions only to be told that Dr. Shim was not available to talk to me. I called to speak to his counselor, *Mr. William Campbell*, and asked him why he told me my son was fine but was lying somewhere in some undisclosed hospital, hidden away from his family and the people who loved him dearly.

He said, "Well, ma'am, the last time I spoke to him he was okay, but when I saw him the last time, oh gheez."

I wanted to ask, *"Oh, gheez, what the hell does that mean?"*

I was getting angrier by the minute and it showed. It showed in my relationships with my family members, my coworkers and my friends. I was desperate! I needed answers and I needed them quick. It became so bad that other people would call for me to check up on Isidro and each time they *too* became frustrated. Peanut would call from Boston and one of the girls on my job would call and pretend she was me in order to keep me from getting too upset at work. Finally, the congressman's office gave the Bureau of Prisons twenty-four hours to tell me where my son was. At the same time, Peanut wrote a letter to Julie Price at the Bureau of Prisons begging for help. The letter asked what condition her brother was in and explained that we just wanted him to know that we loved him and that we wanted to be there with him. She also asked that someone tell him that we loved him and if he was dying, could we please just have a chance to say goodbye. I honestly think that it was that letter that changed the course of things.

Like I said, I was in Pennsylvania when the call finally came in with some real information about Isidro. The call was from Julie Price from the Bureau of Prisons. She left a message on my answering machine stating that she had called with information about Isidro. I had to wait until the next morning to call and I did not sleep at all that night in anticipation of the news. I kept praying to God over and over to please let the news be good. She left a phone number for me to call and as soon as the clock struck 9 a.m., I began to dial the number. When the message came on, it said, *"You have reached the Federal Medical Center in Rochester,"* and before it could finish, I became elated because Rochester was in New York State, but my happiness was short lived. The message continued *"Minnesota."* I was shocked! *Minnesota!* I didn't even know where Minnesota was on the map. The message also sounded cold and impersonal and it sounded like a place where real sick people would be. I waited for the message to continue, *"Push one for this and two for that,"* etc. and when I was finally able to speak to a real person, I was told that the person I needed to speak to would not be in until Monday. All of my frustration came to a head and I began to scream and cry.

I said, "I have been trying to find my son since the 19th of May and now you are telling me that I have to wait until Monday!"

I guess the person on the other end heard the desperation in my voice and told me that he would get someone to call me back. I put the phone down and began to pace back and forth, cursing about *Rochester, Minnesota.*

The phone rang and I snatched it up right way. It was my son's voice! He said, "Hi, Ma." I knew that it was my son but his voice sounded so different, like he was having a very hard time speaking.

The tears started rolling down my cheeks and I said softly, as if not to upset him, "Hi, Isidro, how are you doing?" I was trying to maintain my composure, but his voice sounded so much like his Uncle Willie's when *he* was dying that it took all I had to hold it together. He said that he was okay and then he just stopped talking. The person who had made the call for him took the phone and said something about him having a *"hard time tracking."* I did not know what that meant, but I knew for sure that I did not like the sound of my son's voice. I told the man to tell him that I loved him and that I would be there to see him in a couple of days. I hung up the phone and began to cry so hard that my entire body shook. I had been right. My son *did* need me and I was nowhere around, not even close by. The date was June 13, 1998.

CHAPTER SEVENTEEN

The phone rang again and it was Patti, Lessie's older sister, who was calling to see if I was still going to cook for Dee Dee's birthday party later that day. I began to cry so hard that Patti could not understand what I was saying. I just kept repeating, "Patti, Patti, he is dying."

She asked over and over, "Teresa, what's the matter?"

I got myself together just enough to tell her about the phone call and I could tell by her voice that she did not know what to say. She told me if I did not feel like cooking that she would understand, but I insisted that I would cook and bring the food to the party because I needed something to take my mind off of things. Also, Dee Dee had been through enough in her short life and she needed that party to bring her at least a little happiness if only for the day. Besides, from the sound of her father's voice, I knew in my heart that it would not be long before she had another unhappy event to face that would change the course of her life. Dee Dee was one person who was always making plans for when her dad came home and now it seemed like that was never going to happen. I started cooking the food and prepared for the party knowing that this is what Isidro would have wanted me to do especially since he had never been able to be there for *even one* of Dee Dee's birthdays. I finished cooking the food and then took Sidra and my little cousin Star to the party. I tried my best to keep on a happy face and somehow I made it through the day, but for the life of me, I don't know how I did it. My mind, my body, my heart and my soul were with Isidro and until I could get to him, I would not be able to rest.

CHAPTER EIGHTEEN

It was some time during this period that I stopped going to church on Sundays. I was feeling like God was letting me down and I felt that I had done nothing so bad to deserve this. First, He had taken my son and thrown him in prison and now He was letting him die. It was not right and I just could not go and sit in church. It's what I should have done, but didn't. Instead, I went to the Grotto to pray to the Virgin Mary and to appeal to her as a mother. It was on one of *these* days that I got the first miracle that I had been praying for.

Because of all of the lost days from work and the traveling back and forth to Pennsylvania, I had no money to speak of, certainly not enough to get us all to Minnesota. I had checked with the airlines and found out that it would cost us about five thousand dollars to get there to see Isidro and we had nowhere near that kind of money. This particular afternoon, I took Star and went to the Grotto. It was a Wednesday afternoon *and* the day the rosary group met to pray the *rosary* at the Grotto. I sat down on the benches with the small group of Italian ladies and began to recite the rosary while fingering the rosary beads. The entire time I was praying for the Lord to send a miracle that would allow me to get to

Minnesota to see my son. All of a sudden, my pager went off and the message said 911. I was terrified that it would be Sanyae with a message about Isidro. I did not have a cell phone so I got up and went to look for a pay phone, but there was not one around. I went several places and not one of them had a pay phone. As I often did during this time, I began to cry because it seemed as if nothing was going right. I couldn't even find a pay phone to find out what the emergency was. All of a sudden a man in a *New York City Housing Authority Maintenance* uniform appeared out of nowhere and asked if I was alright. I told him that I really needed to find a telephone. He showed me where the maintenance room was and said that there was a phone right there on the wall next to the door. He said, "Just go in and use it, no one is going to stop you."

I thanked him and hurried to the phone. It was Sanyae saying that her boss had agreed to lend her the money for us to go see about Isidro. I was so happy that I did not know what to say, but when I hung up the phone, I high tailed it back to the Grotto so that I could thank God and the Virgin Mary for answering my prayers, for this was truly a miracle. Before we left to go home, I asked the ladies from the Rosary group to please pray for my son *and* my entire family.

Now that we had the money, we began to make plans to go to Minnesota. We were calling the different airlines to compare rates when my friend Myra suggested that we ask the airlines to give us a compassionate rate. US Airways offered us a greatly discounted fare and we made reservations to travel Friday morning. We called the medical center and found out everything that we had to know so that there would be no problems once we got there. After dealing with the Bureau of Prisons for so long, we knew that anything could happen and we did not want anything to go wrong that would keep us from visiting with Isidro. In addition to the plane ride to Minnesota, there was also a two hour ride from the airport to the medical center. We made reservations with a van service that would take us from the airport to the medical center and then we prayed that everything would go off without a hitch. We took Thursday to make all of the final details of the trip and to make last minute phone calls to make sure that everyone concerned knew that we were coming.

Peanut came in from Boston on Thursday evening and we all made arrangements to meet at my house early the next morning so that we could meet Hector and get to the airport on time. The day was so warm and sunny that it could have looked like we were going on a family vacation. We made it to the airport with time to spare, our flight was on time and the plane ride to Minnesota was uneventful. I have always believed in signs from above and when we arrived at the airport in Minnesota, something happened to me that was surely a sign of things to come. The flight on the plane was rather chilly so I borrowed a jacket from Peanut. As usual, I had my little guardian angel pin attached to my dress and I knew it was there when I got on the plane because I fingered it as I normally did when I was praying for something, and this time it was for us to have a safe flight. When we arrived at the airport in Minnesota, it was very hot, so the first thing I did was take off my jacket. I immediately noticed that my guardian angel pin was missing. I was devastated to say the least. I looked around the area where we were waiting for the van, but it was nowhere to be found. I actually wanted to go back to the plane to find it, but, of course, that was impossible. I was hurt. I knew that my guardian angel was going to be left behind and I felt rather unprotected. I had a really bad feeling that this was a sign of things to come and I could not shake that feeling no matter what I did. Somehow the loss of my guardian angel was a sign from above of what was to come.

We got into the van and tried to enjoy the ride to Rochester, Minnesota. The countryside was beautiful and as I always did when riding to visit my son, I thought of how these prison facilities were all in the same type of places. One would never realize that such a pit of misery could be smack dab in the middle of such a beautiful green and serene countryside. The leaves on the trees blew in the wind giving one the feeling of peace and tranquility. The van driver proudly pointed out several landmarks along the way while the rest of us rode along in silence and apprehension. I don't know about the rest of the family, but I was scared to death. I did not know what we would have to face when we arrived at the institution and at the same time, I was very anxious to see my son. At one point, I had decided not to go at all, but to let my husband and daughters go instead. I was terrified of what I would find when I got there. The anonymous caller had stated that Isidro had passed out in the bathroom and my mind held pictures of him lying on the cold bathroom floor. I did not know if he had injured himself when he fell. I didn't know if he would have any scars from the fall or if, in fact, he had fallen at all. I could not help but wonder what he would look like. Would he be hooked up to any medical apparatus or if he would need any breathing machines like the kind you saw on television. All sorts of pictures kept running through my head. In fact, if it had not been for something my friend Myra had told me, I would not have even gone on the trip at all. I had talked with my friend Myra a couple of days before and I told her that I did not want to go see Isidro because I was afraid. I told her that I was going to send the rest of the family and once they told me what was going on, *then* I would go later.

Myra said, "No, you can't do that. He is your son and you have to go and see about him. Besides, if something were to happen later on down the road, you would never forgive yourself for not going. You have to go and if not for yourself, but for him." To this day I am so glad that Myra told me that because she was right.

CHAPTER NINETEEN

We finally arrived at the Federal Medical Center late that afternoon. On the outside, the building looked like any other small town medical facility, but on the inside it looked cold and foreboding. We waited anxiously while the paperwork was done and, as usual, we played the *hurry up and then wait* game. We sat down and chatted nervously until they finally called our names. We were led through one electronic door after another until we at last reached the visiting room. We again gave our names to the officers on duty and were told to have a seat. I guess they don't realize that the last thing that you want to do is have a seat after you have traveled mile after mile sitting down in cabs, cars, trains and vans. There were only a few other people in the visiting room and I could not help but think that the two tall tattooed inmates sitting across from us looked a lot like the Nazi skinheads that you see on television or in the newspaper. They did not look at all friendly so we chose the seats that were as far across the room as we could get and then sat down to wait some more.

While we were waiting, I could not help but notice that the two guards at the desk were mumbling something to each other and at the same time staring at us, which made me even more uncomfortable. We all kept looking around and wondering which door Isidro would come out of. I was surprised and happy about the fact that we would be sitting in a visiting room instead of at a bedside and I erroneously thought that this must mean that Isidro was not too bad off. We heard a door open and finally Isidro was being wheeled through the door *in a wheelchair!* While we were waiting, we had discussed the fact that whatever happened, we would not do anything to upset Isidro. We would hold back any tears until we got out of his eyesight and it was a good thing because when I saw my son being wheeled into the room in that wheelchair, I wanted to drop to my knees and scream and I am sure that everyone else felt the same way.

My beautiful, strong, healthy son was sitting in a wheelchair obviously wearing an adult diaper. The sight of him in that condition tore at the very fiber of my being. I hugged him but not too tightly as I usually did because I did not want to hurt him in any way. You could see in his eyes that he was very glad to see us and I was surprised that for someone who was so obviously ill that his eyes looked so bright and clear. He looked thin and pale, but he did not look half as bad as I had expected him to look. I did not like the sound of his voice, which was very weak, and he seemed to be having a very hard time speaking. I asked him if he was surprised to see us and was shocked when he said, *"No."* Although he was speaking softly, he told us that the doctor had told him that we had arrived there at eleven that morning which was exactly the time that we had arrived in Minnesota. I also asked him if he remembered what had happened to him and he told us that he had passed out in the bathroom. I was elated that he was able to articulate what had happened and that there was nothing wrong with his mind, a fact which had worried me since I first spoke to the anonymous caller. I asked him if he was cold and he said, *"Yes,"* so we asked one of the officers for a jacket which he readily gave me. We put the jacket on Isidro and I felt better because I could not stand the fact that he seemed cold and was not able to do anything about it. I asked him if he wanted something to drink and he said, *"Yes,"* so I got up and bought him a *Very Fine* juice from the vending machine. I will never, ever forget the way my son drank that juice. His hands were very shaky so we had to hold it for him and he drank the juice so fast that I was worried about him choking or throwing it up. He seemed so satisfied when he finished it that I asked him if he would like another one and he again said, *"Yes."* The second time he drank the juice a little slower and seemed to really enjoy it. We asked him if he wanted anything else from the machine and he said that he wanted a bag of *Fritos.* We got the Fritos for him and again we had to hold them for him because he was unable to hold them for himself. He ate the Fritos like he was very hungry or either because it was a real treat for him. A simple bag of Fritos and a Very Fine juice meant so much to him. I thought about what Myra had said and was very glad that I came to see my son. In the days and months that followed, this scene would play out in my mind a million times.

CHAPTER TWENTY

We left the prison and went to find a place to stay for the night and some food to eat because we were all tired and hungry. We found a little motel that was not too far from the medical center and then went in search of food. Because most of the towns that we had visited during Isidro's incarceration were not prisoner family friendly, we did not dare to venture too far away from the motel and decided on Chinese food, which was the only thing that we could find in walking distance of the motel. We ate the food, watched a little television and then took showers and went to bed. We wanted to be up bright and early the next morning so that we could spend as much time with Isidro as possible before heading home. Before going to sleep, we expressed to one another how we felt about Isidro's condition and we all felt the same way. We all thought that he had been very ill but that he was going to be okay. We said our prayers and went to sleep. *Tomorrow was going to be a better day*, or so we all thought.

Everybody was up early the next morning, but I had beat them to the punch because I wanted to take a long relaxing bath and I did not want to be rushed, so I got up extra early. A long relaxing bath is good before bedtime, but is even better at the start of the day. By the time we were all ready to leave, we had just enough time to get to the medical center for visiting hours. It seemed as if they were expecting us this day because the paperwork did not take half as long as it did the previous day. It was a nice day, but rather cool and the air conditioner was on in the visiting room, so we decided to sit out in the yard in the sun where it was much warmer. While we were waiting for them to bring Isidro in, we got several snacks from the vending machines. After thinking about the juice the day before, I wanted to make sure that he had plenty to eat and drink before we left to go home.

When they brought Isidro into the visiting room, we immediately noticed a change in him. He seemed to be sort of lethargic as if he had been drugged or something. He took longer to answer our questions than he did the day before and he just seemed sort of out of it. He did answer us when we asked him if he wanted something to eat and I was glad that we asked because he again ate like he hadn't eaten in days. This time we got him a pizza from the machine and Sanyae fed it to him piece by piece. He took his time eating this time as if he was savoring every little morsel. In between bites of pizza, he sipped the juice and then went back to the pizza. We were all a little quieter on this day and I guess it was because we were apprehensive about leaving Isidro behind. If I could have been granted one wish that day it would have been to wrap my son up in a warm blanket and take him home with us. Leaving him behind that day was one of the hardest things I have ever had to do in my entire life. If I thought leaving him behind in that courtroom was bad, this was a thousand times worse. On the first day we all came away with a good and positive feeling, but this day we left feeling gloomy and short tempered. We stayed with Isidoro as long as we could but before long it was time to head for the airport. We hugged and kissed Isidoro one by one and then we waited for the C.O's to come to come to get him and take him back to his dorm. I can remember looking at my son who just stared into space. I was looking at him praying to God that he did not shed a tear for if he did it would have been more than I could bear. When we left the institution, all I could do was wonder how my son was going to make it without his family and the people who loved him most. I couldn't understand why he had been taken so far away from home when he needed us more than he ever did in his life. One of the hardest things for me was thinking that my son was thirsty and unable to get a drink and that he was hungry and was unable to get anything to eat. Every time I thought of how he drank that juice it brought tears to my eyes.

We got back to the airport without incident, but on the plane, Hector began to cry and said, "Teresa, you know that we are going to have to bury him soon."

I began to cry too because I had been thinking the same thing.

I no longer had the good feeling about Isidro that we all had the day before. Part of me wanted to bolt from the plane and run all the way back to where my son was. He needed me and I knew it and knowing that I could not be there for him hurt more than words can describe. We were all glad that we had been able to visit Isidro, but the trip back to New York found us all with a feeling of impending doom. I could not wait until I could get to the Grotto again so that I could pray for my son. All of the years that I had been going there I had been praying for my son to be set free, but this was not the kind of freedom that I meant. Now I knew why they said, *be careful what you pray for because you just might get it*. When I arrived home, I kept seeing Isidro guzzling down that juice and somehow I knew that at that very moment he probably needed a cool drink and there was no one there to give it to him. I picked up the telephone and called the Federal Medical Center in Rochester, Minnesota. I begged the nursing staff to please give my son something to drink from time to time for me. When I hung up the phone, I fell to the floor on my knees and began to weep. I cried out loud, "God, help me please!"

CHAPTER TWENTY-ONE

The next few days were hell for me, but somehow I managed to put one foot in front of the other and I was able to get through the days. I guess it had a lot to do with the fact that I was working two jobs and my days were pretty much filled with work and traveling back and forth. On an average day I took two buses and six trains to get to and from work. The nights, however, were a different story. No matter how tired I was at night, I was barely able to sleep. I would come home from work and fall asleep from sheer exhaustion but I did not sleep long. I usually woke up an hour or two later and spent the rest of the night pacing the floor and trying to think of something that I could do to help my son. Most of the time I would wake up and start writing letters to elected officials begging for help for Isidro. The letters were always very emotional and I would usually begin to cry and my tears would fall onto the paper and make the ink run thereby ruining the letter and I would have to start all over again. When morning would come, my eyes would be so red that I looked like I had been out drinking all night. The circles around my eyes were so dark that I started to look like a raccoon. The worse thing for me during this time was when I tried to call and ask how my son was doing or try to get a message to him. The calls were very frustrating because no one wanted to talk to me. One time I called the institution and was connected to a woman named *Jennifer Hoen*. She had to be the rudest and meanest person on earth. She told me in no uncertain terms that she was busy and did not have the time to update me on my son's condition every day. She also went on to tell me that I could call every other week, but that she was certainly not going to take time out of her busy schedule to speak to me every day. When she finished what she had to say, she said goodbye and hung up before I had a chance to say another word. I was standing there with the telephone receiver in my hand and my mouth open as wide as I could. I couldn't believe my ears. She had the nerve to dismiss me when it was *my* son's life that we were talking about. I was thinking that she was a blessed person and that she should thank God above that I was nowhere close to her. At that moment, I wanted to ring her little red neck like a chicken. I guess saying goodbye was her way of not just blatantly hanging up on me. A lot of times I was simply put on hold and no one ever came back to the phone. When I would call back, I would be told that we had been disconnected, but I knew better.

We had been back from Minnesota almost a week when one day, after spending the night praying and pacing the floor, I decided that I was not going to go to work but spend the day trying to get some rest and writing some more letters. I was able to sleep for a couple of hours and then I got up and began to write again. While I was sitting at the kitchen table writing another letter to President Clinton, my mind began to wander back to the time when I first began writing to presidents. I was in the third grade and we were given a homework assignment to write a letter to the president. Everyone in the class had to do this and I remembered how excited we all were when our answers began to come in. I was one of the first persons in the class to get my response and it made me an instant celebrity. From that time, whenever I had a problem, I would write the president and I always received an answer and that is why I was so disappointed when I never received an answer from President Clinton. I started writing him about Isidro as soon as he took office and I have never, not even once, received an answer. In fact, I have never received an answer from Hillary Clinton even though she is the senator from New York State.

Ricky came home from school while I was writing the letters and once he saw me writing, he retired to his room. Ricky was a child that never stopped talking from the time he learned how to talk, but when Isidro became ill, he had become unusually quiet. He would come home from school, immediately sense my mood and would go to his room and not aggravate me as he normally did. One particular day he came in and asked if I had heard anything about Isidro and I told him no. During this period, no news was good news. Ricky was watching television when the phone rang and he ran to answer it. Lately, every time the phone would ring, I would literally jump out of my chair and one of Ricky's ways of helping out was to get the phone right away.

He answered the phone and said, "Ma, it's Deloris from your job."

I took the phone expecting her to ask me how I was doing, but instead she said, "Teresa, are you sitting down?"

As soon as she said that, I expected the worst. I screamed into the phone, "What happened?"

She said, "Don't get excited."

She had just asked me if I was sitting down and now she was telling me not to get excited. How could I *not* get excited?

Deloris went on to say that the doctor had called from the medical center and he told her that the news was not good.

I screamed into the phone, "Deloris, is my son dead?"

She said, "No," but there was something about the way she said it that I did not like.

I began to scream so Ricky took the phone from me and started speaking to Deloris. He then handed the phone back to me and said, "Ma, Isidro is not dead. Here, talk to Deloris because she has a message from the doctor."

I took the phone and listened as Deloris detailed her conversation with Dr. Tran from the Federal Medical Center in Rochester, Minnesota. He told Deloris that Isidro had been taken to the Mayo Clinic and that I could come to see him if I wanted to. I don't know how I could have felt any worse, but I did when I recalled one conversation with Dr. Tran. He told me that Isidro was being taken care of, but if anything should happen, he would be immediately taken to the Mayo Clinic, which was close to the Medical Center. I could not imagine how things could get any worse, but I needed to talk to this doctor myself. I thanked Deloris for giving me the message and then immediately tried to reach Dr. Tran. I was on hold waiting for Dr. Tran when there was a loud knock on my door. Ricky answered it and there were two police officers standing there. Even though they were friends of mine from work, I began to cry again because I was sure that they were there to give me bad news. They came in and assured me that they were only there because they were sent there by the lieutenant to stand by me should the news get worse. I was so glad that they were there because I did not know if Ricky could handle it if things did get worse. Ricky offered the officers a seat and it was easy to see that they were as nervous as I was and that they did not know what to say to me. We sat making small talk and Ricky offered them some chocolate chip cookies and water. I found this kind of comical and asked Ricky why he offered them cookies and *water* and he said because that was all we had in the house.

I thought about this and I could not remember the last time I had gone grocery shopping. Poor Ricky, I am sure he was suffering through all of this. He did not even get much attention when he had his surgery because I was too worried about his brother and I am sure that he was worried about him too.

The officers did not mind the cookies and water too much and were kind enough to sit with me for quite a while. When I finally got in touch with Dr. Tran, he was very vague about what had gone wrong with Isidro. In fact, what he said in no way prepared me for what was to come. Because I had no idea of the seriousness of what had happened, I went back to work and continued calling to check on my son. One night I was at work when I got a call from Lessie's sister Patty. She was calling for something else, but she asked me about Isidro. When I told her how seriously ill he was, she asked me what I was doing at work and why wasn't I in Minnesota with Isidro. I told her that since we just came back from there, I did not have enough money to go again. She told me not to worry, that she would buy me a plane ticket and that I should get ready to go back immediately. I was so happy I did not know what to do. So many miracles had happened since Isidro got sick and God had put so many good people in my life when I needed them to be there.

I went home from work, very happy that I would get to see my son again. I packed and waited for Patty to arrange the flight. We were able to get a compassionate rate flight from US Airways that only cost three hundred thirty-three dollars round trip. *Talk about a blessing.* I spent Sunday night in anticipation of seeing my son again. It meant a lot to me because since the last trip I had worried about him constantly. I would always picture him drinking that juice like he had not had anything to drink in weeks, which could have very well been the case. I promised myself that when I got there I would give him anything that he asked for as long as I was there. I did not know how long I would be staying there, but I knew that I would be there as long as he needed me. I had enough money to pay for the van trip, a couple of days at a motel and some food. I did not care about the food because I had not had an appetite for days, so food was not on my list of priorities.

When Monday morning came, I was excited and nervous at the same time. I was up hours before my plane was scheduled to leave, and when Myra came to give me a ride to the airport, I was ready. I was glad that Myra was able to give me a ride because I knew that she would be talking and it would keep my mind off of things. I had been afraid to go to see Isidro the first time even though I had the whole family with me, but this time, I did not have that feeling of fear even though I was going all alone. Since I had been there only days before, I knew that I would remember my way around. The hardest part would be getting from the airport to the hospital where Isidro had been taken a couple of days earlier. I did not know where the Mayo Clinic was, but I knew that once I got into the state of Minnesota, there would be no keeping me from finding my son this time. Where I was getting the courage from, I did not know.

Myra was on time and we got to the airport without getting stuck in traffic, which was the first miracle of the day. Myra did not feel like hanging around the airport and left as soon as I got to the *check in* counter. I really wanted her to stay there with me, but there was no way that I could make her stay. As soon as she left, I sat down and tried to read the newspaper. Instead of reading the paper, I became lost in thought. I started wondering what had gone wrong in life for Isidro and what brought us to the point that we were at now. *How could this have happened? What had gone wrong inside those prison walls that had my strong healthy son not able to even hold a cup of water for himself? Why did the Bureau of Prisons hide him away from us for so long? Why did they lie to me and tell me that my son had walked off of the plane in Minnesota when he got there.* When we saw him the last time, it was obvious that he had not walked anywhere for some time. I intended to get some answers on this trip. I would not let the officials from the Bureau of Prisons push me around any longer. They owed me an explanation and I intended to get it. Every time something came up with Isidro, I would be very careful about what I said or did because he had let me know early on that if you pissed them off in any way, they would not hesitate to take it out on your loved ones. I thought about this all through the years and with Isidro in this helpless condition, I really did not want to do anything to cause them to retaliate against Isidro in any way. I always worried about him, but I took some comfort in the fact that he had always been able to hold his own. This thought brought me back to the time when Isidro was in a football game out in the snow in front of the building across the street from us.

I had been watching the game from the window for quite some time when all of a sudden a fight broke out. I could see one figure lying on the ground and another figure on top of him pounding away. I looked closely and spotted Isidro's jacket. I asked my cousin, Madeline, if that was in fact Isidro on the ground.

She looked out of the window and said, "Yes, it is him, and why is he letting that boy beat on him like that?"

I opened up the window and shouted for Isidro to get up and fight back. He still did not move, so I grabbed my coat and Madeline and I ran down the stairs to find out what was gong on. When we got across the street, Isidro was still lying on the ground and the boy was still punching him in the face. One thing you did not do if you lived in the projects was to let someone hit you and not hit back because to do that would be an open invitation for everyone to do whatever they wanted to you.

I was so mad that I leaned over and said, "Isidro, what the hell is wrong with you? Get up and hit him back!"

Isidro looked up and said, "Ma, I do not want to fight him because I know I can beat him and it is no fun fighting someone you can beat." He then looked up at the boy and said, "I'm getting cold, now let me up."

The boy continued to pound away at Isidro's face and the redder his face became, the angrier *I* got. Finally, I said, "Isidro, if you don't get up and fight back, I am going to kick your ass too."

Isidro then told the boy, "This is the last time I am going to ask you to let me up."

It was the last time too because before the young man had a chance to think about it, Isidro drew back his fist and slammed it into the side of the boy's head. Blood flew into the snow and the blows began to rain on his head. I know that kid was sorry he did not let Isidro up when he asked him to. It would have surely saved him from the beating he got.

As we were walking away, Isidro looked back at the boy nursing his bloody and swollen nose and said, "Now, maybe the next time someone tells you they don't want to fight, you might listen."

Isidro was always one to walk away from a fight or an argument and he always knew how to handle himself, that is, until he got into the hands of the Bureau of Prison officials. Lord only knows what they put my child through.

CHAPTER TWENTY-TWO

I was so lost in thought that I did not even hear the announcement for my flight being called. When I went to the information counter I was told that my flight had been delayed so the passengers were being transferred to another flight in another terminal. I was also told that the new flight was leaving soon and that I should hurry up and get to the terminal. I went down stairs to find the airport shuttle that would take me to the terminal and found out that the next one leaving would not get me to the terminal in time to catch my flight. I got directions and decided to take a few shortcuts through the parking lots so that I could get there on time. I was carrying one of those old suitcases without wheels and it was hard to try to maneuver the suitcase and run too. The visits to see Isidro through the years had taught me a lot about traveling by car, but nothing about traveling by airplane. I have since learned what to take and what not to take when traveling by air.

I finally made it to the terminal all out of breath and huffing and puffing from the run over. I had barely made it to the check in counter when the flight began to board. I took my seat and began to say my airplane prayer. I was not at all scared or anxious about the plane. I was thinking that I was going to see my son and that was all that mattered. If I did not make it for some reason, then I would have nothing to worry about. I thought about this for a minute and knew that nothing was going to happen because God was not going to take me away from my son, not now anyway. I was pleased to learn that the flight I was on was a non-stop flight and I would now get into Minnesota sooner than I had planned. This meant that I would get to see Isidro even sooner than I had planned. I sat back and began to enjoy the flight and my mind began to wander back to Isidro again.

Isidro was a little boy who loved the snow. He would look out of the window every time the snow started to fall and pray for a real snowstorm, the kind that made the schools close and the buses stop running. If there was enough snow, he would go outside and slide down the hill in front of our building, and if it had snowed really hard, he would grab his shovel and head out to make some money shoveling snow. He was never afraid of a little hard work and was always eager to make a little spending money on his own. A lot of times I had to go looking for him because when he got outside in the snow, he lost track of time and I would go out and find him in a snow pile wet from head to toe. And as much as Isidro loved the snowy winters, he loved the summers even more. As soon as the weather reached fifty degrees, he would get out his shorts. We used to say *never listen to Isidro when it comes to the temperature because everything was hot to him*. Once we were taking him to school and his father looked out of the window and asked him how the weather was outside. He said, "It's hot, you do not need a jacket." Needless to say, we both went out without jackets and nearly froze to death. After that, we never listened to Isidro when it came to the weather.

Isidro was just like a fish when it came to water. When he

was small, we would have a time getting him to take a bath. He never wanted to stop what he was doing to take a bath, but once you got him into the bathtub, it was twice as hard to get him out. Isidro was not a child to make a lot of noise so it was not unusual when you did not hear from him for a while and when he was taking a bath, it was no different. After a while I would ask where he was and someone would answer, "He is still in the bathtub."

I would say, "Boy, get out of that tub before you shrivel up and go down the drain with the bath water."

His normal bath time was at least an hour or more. He is the only one I know who could turn a housing project bathtub into a swimming pool.

Another thought I had of Isidro was the way he brought anything and anybody home for his mother to take care of. It did not matter if it was a dog or a cat or a human being, but he always had someone for me to feed and take care of. I remember one boy he brought home and it took us almost two years to get rid of him. His name was Orin, but for some unknown reason, they called him Knowledge, but it definitely was not because he was smart. They brought Knowledge home one evening and told me that his mother had passed away and that his father was in prison and he was living in a group home and that he could not go back there because the kids were going to beat him up. There had evidently been a dispute over a pair of shoes and the kids were afraid of Knowledge getting jumped if he went back to the group home. Well, I gave Knowledge a good hot meal and sent him on his way. A few hours later, Isidro said that he had to go and get Knowledge because the kids had in fact jumped him. Isidro went to the group home and I became an unofficial foster mother. Knowledge was not at all like Isidro and after he settled in with the kids, he started to change the rules.

When the rest of the kids went to school, Knowledge, without my knowledge, would go and hang out and then come home at the end of the school day with the rest of the children. And, forget about taking a bath. Knowledge was like a cat when it came to water...he was afraid of it. One day I told him to drop everything and get into the tub and by the tone of my voice, he knew I meant it, or so I thought. I was listening to the sound of the running water and realized that it had been running steady for at least ten minutes. Not the kind of sound like when someone is taking a bath where there is splashing or movement in the tub, so I decided to open the door and see exactly what was going on. Well, to my surprise, there was Knowledge sitting on the side of the tub with his chin in his hand looking like he had lost his best friend. I had had enough. I reached over, pushed Knowledge into the bathtub, clothes and all and said, "Now, you can take a bath *and* wash your clothes at the same time."

I couldn't figure out why I was putting myself through this when I already had four kids of my own and I was not getting paid one red cent. After a year and a half, I decided to give Knowledge an ultimatum. He would either go to school or he could go back to the group home. It was his choice, but I was not going to continue to go out and work to support a kid who did not belong to me and who would not do the one thing I asked and that was to go to school and make something out of himself. Knowledge chose to go back to the group home where he could sleep late and hang out as long as he wanted and still get fed too.

Isidro also brought home a couple of special needs animals too. He once had two parakeets, a male and a female. The female pecked at the male's head until he hadn't any more feathers, but little spots of blood. One morning I woke up to find Isidro quite upset because he found the male lying at the bottom of the birdcage stiff and still and not breathing. He felt that if he had gotten up during the night he could have somehow saved the bird's life.

He also had a little white mouse that he called *Charlie* who lasted for a good while until the dog got a hold of him one day when Isidro was cleaning out his cage. I did not mind Isidro's animals too much, it was just the people that he brought home that caused the most problems. Isidro always had a soft spot for anyone or anything that needed to be taken care of. This need to take care of people followed him to prison too.

One day he called and said that there was a young boy from the New York area that was getting out and needed a place to stay. My first impulse was to tell him that he must be out of his damn mind, but I just said that I would see what I could do. Against my better judgment, I said that I would give it a try, but when the Bureau of Prisons started calling my house and harassing me, I decided that I had enough on my plate and the last thing that I needed was to have to answer to the Bureau of Prisons for someone that I did not even know.

I was lost in thought when the stewardess stopped by to ask me if I wanted something to drink. I guess she thought I was asleep which was why she had to tap me lightly on the shoulder to get my attention. I said that I would take some water and then put my head back and continued to scan through the wonderful years that I shared with my beautiful son.

I guess I must have fallen asleep from sheer exhaustion because all of a sudden I heard the *fasten your seat belt* announcement and soon after we landed at the Minneapolis St. Paul airport. I gathered up my bags and went immediately to the area where I would get the van that would take me to the Mayo Clinic. It seemed like the closer I got to the hospital, the more nervous I became. Although there was only a short line at the reservation counter, I became very impatient. It seemed like everything was taking so long. When my turn came, the reservation clerk took my name, collected my money and gave me instructions to the gate where my van would be waiting. I was annoyed when I learned that the van was not going straight to the hospital but was to make several stops along the way. The ride to the hospital did not seem to take as long as it did the first time and I guess this was because the route was slightly familiar to me. I tried to calm my nerves by enjoying the scenery and reading the newspaper and I guess it worked because before long, we were pulling up in front of the Mayo Clinic. I could not help but notice how clean everything was in the area. The streets were immaculate as were the hospital grounds. The flowers were in full bloom and the landscaping around the hospital was beautiful. The atmosphere was so beautiful that my mood immediately began to brighten.

Before I left New York, I had been given the name and telephone number of a prison official to call when I got to the hospital, but the gentleman was one step ahead of me all the way. I had called him from the airport to let him know that I arrived and I guess he knew exactly what time I would reach Rochester because he was waiting for me when I got to the hospital. He was very pleasant and took me straight to see my son after asking a few questions about my flight and the time it took me to get there. We took the elevator to the fifth floor and walked down a long corridor until we got to my son's room. There was a prison guard standing outside of the door who just nodded to us as we walked in and I was surprised to see a female guard sitting inside. I was thinking what a waste of taxpayer's money to have two officers guarding an inmate who was obviously not going anywhere. When I saw my son, I could not believe my eyes! He was propped up on some pillows and appeared to be sleeping. What really shocked me was the fact that he looked so good. He did not look at all like he did when we last saw him. His skin complexion was nice and rosy and his face looked like it did on the day he was first arrested. I took a few steps and went around to get a better look at him before I woke him up. With the exception of the IV tubes, there were no machines or medical apparatuses hooked up to him. The sight of him lying there, looking so good and so peaceful, made me want to jump for joy. I knew he would be glad to see me so I tapped him gently on the shoulder and whispered his name. I did this a couple of times before he turned his head towards me and opened his eyes. He kind of looked at me and rolled his eyes, turned his head away and appeared to fall back asleep. At first I did not know what to think and then I asked myself if he could be angry at me for some unknown reason. No, Isidro would not roll his eyes at his mother and turn away, especially after he knew that she had come so far to see him. I called to him again and asked, "Isidro, aren't you glad to see me?"

The female guard did not say anything, but the male guard said, "It's funny, but he does not seem to respond to too much of anything, but when the soccer game comes on, he pays attention."

I said, "No, this cannot be happening." *What does he mean Isidro only pays attention to the soccer game?* I tried a couple of more times and each time he sort of looked past me as if he could hear my voice but was not sure exactly where it was coming from. It is a miracle that I did not drop dead from a heart attack right there and then. Now I knew why that doctor told my coworker that the news was not good. No one told me anything like this was going on. I thought to myself, *"These assholes have been telling me that my son was fine and now look at this."*

I remembered speaking to his counselor about his eyesight long ago and him telling me something about an eye doctor's appointment. I even wrote to Kathleen Hawk, the Director of the Bureau of Prisons, expressing my concerns about my son's eyesight and I had been given the royal brush off, and now he was lying in this hospital bed very obviously not able to see me and here were two idiots talking about him *watching the soccer games*. At that moment I wanted to kill someone. Before I had a chance to digest everything, the gentleman who escorted me into the hospital said that I had to leave because visiting hours were over. I really did not want to leave my son, but I needed to get out of there and find a hotel or motel room so that I could sit down and collect my thoughts. I wanted to scream and cry, but I knew that this was not the time *or* the place to break down. At that moment I knew that I had made a grave mistake by making this trip alone. I kissed Isidro on his forehead, stroked his hand for a few minutes and then I let the prison official lead me down the corridor to the bank of elevators and then out into the street.

I don't know what he was thinking at that moment, but I am sure that my feelings must have shown in my face because the kind of emotions that I was feeling were hard to hide. I can vaguely remember him saying something about me being able to visit the next day, and I guess I told him that I was going to find a motel room because soon he was walking one way and I was standing on the street in a daze. It was one of those times when you get strength that you did not know you had because somehow I was able to keep the focus and remember what it was that I was supposed to do next. I looked up and down the street and was able to see a motel sign from where I was standing. I headed in that direction and soon came to a motel that had a vacant sign. I went inside and inquired about the rates and was told that there was only one room left and that it was a no smoking room.

I told the clerk that I would take the room and handed him my credit card. I took the keys and my bags and followed his directions and made it to the room. When I got inside and closed the door, I just dropped my bags on the floor, fell down on my knees and began to sob. The cries did not come from my mouth or my eyes, but from somewhere deep down inside of me. I don't know how long I stayed like that, but the ringing of the telephone brought me back to earth and I ran to pick it up although I could not imagine who would be calling me because I had not even called to let my family know that I had arrived. When I answered the telephone, it was the gentleman who had escorted me into the hospital. I guess being an agent it was not hard for him to find out where I was staying. He asked me what time I would be going to the hospital the following morning and when I told him he then made arrangements to meet me there. I hung up the phone and thought to myself, *"It's going to be a long night."* And I was right.

I tried to pull myself together enough to think straight. I did not know in what direction to turn. I did not know who to call or what to say if I did call someone. I had to call and let my family know that I had arrived in Rochester, Minnesota, safely although I really wanted to wait until I had more information about Isidro to tell them. I took a deep breath, picked up the phone, called home, let them know that I had seen Isidro and I was immediately asked how he was doing. When I told them that he looked much better, they said good and asked what he said. This was the question that I did not want to answer. I lied and said that he was sleeping when I got there and I did not want to wake him up. Knowing me, I am sure that they found this very hard to believe, but I thought that it would be best if I waited until I had more information to give them. After assuring them that I was alright, I said goodnight, and hung up the phone. At that moment, I did not know what to do with myself. I had not eaten all day but I was not at all hungry. I decided to go outside and smoke a cigarette since there was nothing else to do and my nerves were so much on edge that the walls felt like they were closing in on me. I put on my shoes, grabbed my cigarettes and walked outside.

From the front of the motel, I could see that there was a *Super A* gas station within walking distance so I decided to take a stroll over there and see if I could find something to occupy my mind and my time. I walked over there and bought a couple of bottles of water and was waiting in line when my eyes fell on some lottery scratch tickets. I got a couple of the tickets, paid for the water and headed back to the motel. I went back to the motel, took off my clothes, sat down and began scratching the tickets. About fifteen minutes later I had scratched all of the tickets and had won ninety dollars. I was very happy about this because I had a limited amount of money, but instead of keeping the money, I put aside what I had started with, got dressed again and went back to the Super A. I bought some more tickets and began scratching them before I got back to the motel. When I won a few more bucks, I turned around and went back for more tickets. Each time I would put aside the amount of money that I started with and then I would go back again for more tickets. I did this about eight or ten times, just walking back and forth between the motel and the Super A. On my last trip back to the gas station, I noticed a green pick up truck on the opposite side of the street rolling along slowly. The man driving the truck waved to me and smiled. I waved back and smiled too because I knew that this was something that people in small towns did, but I began to get nervous when the truck followed me into the Super A parking lot. I got my last batch of tickets and high-tailed it back to the motel. I ran inside, locked the door and put the chain lock on. Being from New York City, I just assumed that the man had been watching me and thought that I was *looking for something to do* and *somebody to do it with*, and I could see how it must have looked that way from his point of view with me walking back and forth to the gas station so many times. I had my share of problems and Lord knows I did not need any more, so I decided to call it a night. I don't know how long I would have walked back and forth if that truck did not start following me. It was just 11 o'clock and I had a long night ahead of me.

I turned on the TV set and decided to watch the news and see what was happening in Minnesota, and after a few minutes I lost interest in that too. I guess that was when my mind started to wander and I began thinking of my once strong and healthy son who was now lying in a hospital bed, just a couple of blocks away, and here I was with nothing to do and I was not allowed to be by his side where I needed to be. I was trying very hard not to be angry because being angry kept me from thinking straight. All I wanted to do right then was to run the few blocks to the hospital, take my son in my arms, hold him and tell him that I loved him. When I saw him earlier that day, he seemed sort of feverish and I would have loved to have been able to sponge his head and make sure he was comfortable. I thought of the time when he was little and he was in the hospital. I had been visiting my mother when Isidro got into her cleaning fluids and had to be suddenly rushed to the hospital. We weren't sure if he got to drink any or not, but they decided to pump his stomach out anyway. It was a terrible feeling watching him lie there and not being able to comfort him, but I knew that what they were doing was necessary and once they were finished, he was going to be okay. This time was different. I was not allowed to be a part of the decision making process and I was not allowed to be there to comfort him. In fact, I was not allowed to be there at all. I did not know which was worse, being in Minnesota, a few blocks away or being in New York City, miles away. Knowing he was just a few blocks away made me want to run to the hospital, demand to be let in and just be there, hoping he knew that I was there by his side.

I guess I must have fallen asleep because the ringing of the phone woke me up. It was the gentleman from the Bureau of Prisons who met me at the hospital the night before. He wanted to know what time I was coming to the hospital and I told him that I would be there as soon as I showered and dressed. He went on to say that there was a problem and that he would have to see me before I went in to visit Isidro. My heart stopped for a minute and I asked him if anything had happened to Isidro during the night. He said no but I was not convinced because I had been lied to and misled from the beginning. I told him I would be there in a few minutes and I hung up the phone and rushed to get ready to meet him in the hospital lobby. When I got there, he was waiting for me and began to explain to me that he should have not let me in the hospital the way he did the night before. He said that I was supposed to first go to the Rochester Medical Center and fill out a visiting form and then I would be allowed to visit. Although it was early in the morning, it was already warm, but when he said this, my blood began to boil. *Why on God's earth should I have to go to the medical center, which was all the way across town, when Isidro was right here in the hospital?* This made no sense and besides that, I was sure that it would be expensive to get there and back. Like in everything with the Bureau of Prisons, I had no choice but to go along with this because it was the only way that I was going to be allowed to see my son. I could see that this was not going to be a good day even though the sun was shining, and from all appearances, all was right with the world.

The prison official gave me the telephone number of a cab that I could call that would take me directly to the medical center for fifteen dollars. That would be thirty dollars round trip and I definitely did not have thirty dollars to waste. I began to think that all of these people were in cahoots and that the cab company must be getting a kick back because this was the most asinine thing that I had heard that year, going all the way to the medical center just to fill out a visiting form for someone that was not even there. When the cab came, I got in, sat down and began to cry. After seven-and-a-half years, the Bureau of Prisons had begun to wear me down. From the beginning, I promised that I would be strong for my son's sake, but I did not know how much more I could take. I just couldn't imagine what it must have been like for the inmates if they treated the family like this. The cab driver looked in the rearview mirror and asked if I was okay and that is when the floodgates really opened up. I told him all about what had happened to my son and how it took me twenty-two days just to find out where he was and now that I was finally there, they were still sticking the screws to me by making me go out to the institution to fill out a stupid visiting form. I told him that I did not know how long I was going to have to be there and that I just did not have the money to be going back and forth, which was the reason I got a motel room within walking distance of the Mayo Clinic. The cab driver said he knew exactly what I meant because he had heard that *and* worse from the family members of inmates that he had driven to and from the institution. He felt so bad for me that he agreed to bring me back for free. When we reached the prison medical center, the cab driver waited outside while I went in to fill out the visiting forms. He told me that he would be circling around because they would not allow him to sit in front and wait for me. I got inside of the building and got the shock of my life.

There, standing in the lobby, was the very same person that met me at the Mayo Clinic that morning and told me that I had to go to the prison hospital to fill out a visiting form. I was flabbergasted! *Why on earth did he make me come all of the way out here just to fill out a visiting form that he could have just as easily brought to the Mayo Clinic?* If I thought I was angry before, what I was now feeling was past angry. *Why were they doing this to me? Was it not enough that they had allowed my son to get so sick that he might not make it or were they trying to kill me off too?* It took every ounce of whatever I had inside to go over to the visiting desk, fill out the form and then leave gracefully. I suppose what I was thinking showed in my face because the prison official started explaining that it was against Bureau of Prison policy for him to drive me over there. I wanted to tell him that he could take his prison policy and shove it up his ass, but I just smiled at him and left.

It must have been my anger that kept me from boohooing all the way back to the Mayo Clinic. The cab driver was nice and even gave me a receipt for my round trip fare when I only paid him for one way. My day had gotten off to a very bad start and I had no way of knowing at the time that it would get much worse.

CHAPTER TWENTY-THREE

I went into the hospital and very easily found my way back to Isidro's room although I had only been there once before. I guess it is a mother's instinct to find her child. As soon as I walked into the room, the female officer picked up a cell phone and called someone as she had done the night before. The other officer set in on me before I even had a chance to get both feet into the room. He told me that it was not a good idea for me to bring my pocketbook with me to the hospital. My patience was wearing thin and I asked him where I could leave it. What I really wanted to ask him was where did his mother leave her pocketbook when she was going out? Maybe I could leave it there! I told him that it was the only way that I could carry my money, my keys and my personal items. It was not until months later that I discovered that I was carrying a knife in that pocketbook. It was a little red folding knife with a can opener that a police officer had given me years earlier and that I did not even realize was in the pocketbook. I sat the pocketbook down on the floor, a good distance away from both the hospital bed and the correction officers and that was the best I could do at the moment. I walked over to my son's bed and gently shook him to see if he was asleep. Again, he turned in my direction but did not appear to either see or hear me. I had hoped that he had been given some sort of medication the night before and that today he would open his eyes and acknowledge my presence. This did not happen. He just opened his eyes and stared blankly at the ceiling. I wanted to break down and cry but I did not want to give the correction officers the satisfaction of seeing this happen. I just grabbed my son's hand and began to talk to him, which was hard to do with those two officers staring in my face. He still felt a little feverish so I wet a washcloth and placed it on his head. I continued to rub his hand and talk to him even though it seemed as if he did not know that I was there. I stayed there until I couldn't hold back my tears any longer. At the same time, the nurse came in to change his bedding.

The night before I had left some rosary beads with him, but they were not around his neck now. I asked the correction officer about them and she said that she would ask the nurse. When the nurse came in, I asked her myself and she said that she would look around for them. I somehow knew that it was going to be the guards and not the nurses that would discover what had happened to the beads, and I was very annoyed at the fact that they were not at his beside where I had left them. *What did they think? Did they think I was going to smuggle a gun in to him in a rosary bead?* The nurse came in with an armful of sheets, towels and washcloths and I knew it was time for her to give Isidro his morning care. Just as she sat the linen down on the foot of the bed, Isidro sort of turned and his right foot slipped from under the sheet. It was at that moment I knew that my strength was coming from God and that it was He that was guiding me because if I did not lose it at that moment, I never would. I did not know what I had been thinking about, but Isidro was barely able to move and it was obvious to anyone with eyes that he was not going anywhere, but when his foot slipped from under the sheet, I could see that he was shackled to the bed. I had to get out of that room and away from those correction officers as fast as I could. Seeing my child, in his helpless condition, shackled to that bed, did something to me. There is a part of each one of us that has something in us that nobody knows about and most of the time will never know about. Well, I have it in me too and I know that at that moment, God told me to get out of that room and to get out fast and that is what I did. Without another word or a backward glance, I flew out of that hospital and into the street where I was hoping God's sun would shine on me and revitalize me because I was running out of steam.

I went outside and took a couple of deep breaths and then began to take a slow walk around the hospital grounds. A long casual walk always did wonders for me. It was like some form of therapy, as if I were being energized by the sun. I just strolled around the grounds and after a while, my mind began to wander again. I had only walked a couple of blocks, but I was out of breath as if I had run for miles. I was becoming mentally exhausted and I knew if something did not happen fast, I would not be able to go on alone. I had to pull myself together immediately because I had to help my son. I was praying for him to open his eyes and see me or for him to hear me and know that I was there. I did not want him to wake up and see me falling apart. I came upon a bench on the hospital grounds and sat down to pray. I was saying, *"God, I know that I have not been a saint, but please don't let my son suffer for my sins. God, if you have to take someone, take me, but please don't take my child. He has his whole life ahead of him. He has young children."* I got out my rosary beads and began praying to the Virgin Mary, appealing to her as a mother. I kept saying over and over, *"God, please help my child."* I thought of all of the good things that Isidro had done in his life. I thought of his daughters and the many other people who loved him. I thought of his father and how he had just lost both of his brothers in a short span of time. I thought of his sisters and his brother who had suffered with him through all of the years of his incarceration. Most of all, I thought of Isidro lying in that hospital unaware that I was there by his side and unable to respond to my voice or my touch. I guess I just sat there in a trance until a noise from the street brought me out of it and I stood up and began to walk back toward the hospital. Even though I was in a hurry to get back to my son, my shoes felt like they were lined with lead, making it harder to move one foot in front of the other.

When I got back to the room, Isidro was all washed and shaved and his bed had fresh linen. I felt very pleased that the doctors and nurses at the Mayo Clinic were giving him the best of care. They seemed genuinely concerned and this took a little of the load off of my mind. Remembering how thirsty he had been in the Federal Medical Center, I could hardly believe that he would have been given any kind of decent care in there. Having to think of your child lying in his own waste, unable to get any attention or call out for help does not make a parent feel good.

Again, as soon as I walked into the room, the female officer picked up the cell phone to call whoever it was that she would notify each time I came into the room. She would dial the number and spend the next few minutes whispering into the phone. I could not hear what she was saying nor did I care. My main and *only* concern at the time was the welfare of my child who was lying in that bed and I was not getting any answers. I asked to speak to a doctor and was told that I had to speak to the prison doctor and not the doctors who were attending to Isidro at the Mayo Clinic. I was also told that I would have to call *Dr. Tran*, the same doctor who constantly kept me on hold when I would call from New York City. I thought to myself that I was going to speak to the doctors who were available regardless of what she had to say. I was determined to speak to one of the Mayo Clinic doctors and I hatched a plan to leave the room when they came in to see Isidro and then meet them in the hall on their way out. This was not going to be easy because in addition to the guard inside of the room, there was one standing or sitting outside of the room at all times. Right then I did not give a damn if they had *fifty* guards stationed around that room. My son was lying there helpless and I was going to speak to a doctor to find out exactly what was going on regardless of what they had to say about it.

I guess they were expecting me to do something like that because when the doctors finished discussing Isidro's case, the officer followed me out into the hallway. I stopped one doctor and asked him what was going on with my son, but before he had a chance to explain, the officer got in the middle and said that he would answer my questions. The doctor said thank you and walked away to continue with his morning rounds. I was extremely annoyed, but also determined. I made up my mind that the next time I would corner one of the doctors in a way that I would get answers. You just had to be one step ahead of those federal people.

I went back into my son's room and sat at his bedside. It was very hard to just sit there and look at him and not be able to help him in any way. I would feel his head and if he felt warm, I would go to the bathroom and soak a washcloth in cold water and then place it on his forehead. I could not tell if he had a fever or if he was feeling warm from the temperature in the room, but it made me feel good to do something for him, anything, just as long as I was doing something for my son, no matter how little it was. I noticed that each time I moved, it appeared that I made the correction officer nervous, so to break the monotony, I made a game of it. Each time they would get comfortable, I would jump up suddenly and either go into the bathroom or go out of the room or I would just jump up from the chair and go over to Isidro and rub his hands or sponge his forehead. The few words that I did say to him I said very softly because I did not want to share the few words that I had for my son with the officers. I actually enjoyed making them nervous. I guess it is true that misery loves company because I was truly miserable at the time. I would get up and leave the room to go downstairs to the chapel to pray or I would just go to the vending machines to get a drink and them come back, but whatever I did, you could tell that they did not like my sudden movements. Maybe it was the fact that they could not tell me when to sit down or get up that bothered them so much, but whatever it was, it definitely bothered them both and I enjoyed every moment of it.

I was well into my game of cat and mouse when the doctors returned to see Isidro that afternoon. One of the doctors looked at Isidro and mumbled something about how sad his case was and mentioned to the other doctors that I was his mother. There was a female doctor there from the infectious disease department who was obviously not aware of the fact that Isidro was an inmate because she turned to me and asked me if Isidro had been around cats lately. *I finally had my chance.* Before the guards got a chance to protest, I jumped up from my seat by Isidro's beside and began asking questions. The guard was fuming, but when she attempted to interrupt, I simply said, *"Excuse me,"* and kept talking to the doctor.

One doctor looked at me with pity in his eyes and took my hand and said, "Ma'am, your son is dying. He is dying and the process has already started."

I felt as if he had punched me in the chest. I had expected

bad news but not this. My mouth flew open but no words would come out. Even the sassy little corrections officer did not say a word and to this day I thank God that she didn't say anything at that moment. I think she was sort of in shock at the directness of the doctor. The doctor went on to say that it could take a few days, a week, or a month, but that he was dying and there was nothing anyone could do about it. I just stood there silently with the tears rolling down my cheeks. *My son was dying! Why?* A few short months ago he had been strong and healthy and then *bang!* Everything started going downhill, and fast too.

When I was able to speak, I asked the doctor what he was dying from. I said, "What is my son dying from? AIDS does not kill people, it's the infections or pneumonia or something else, but not AIDS."

The doctor looked at me with a questioning expression and then said, "AIDS, who said anything about AIDS?" I guess the officer had recovered because before the doctor got to say another word, she jumped up from her seat with the cell phone to her ears and yelled, "I told you that you were not to speak to these doctors! I told you more than once that you are to speak to Dr. Tran and Dr. Tran only and if you insist on speaking to these doctors, you will be removed from this hospital immediately!"

My chest felt like the doctor had plunged a knife into it and she was now twisting it. The pain was unbearable. I began to hyperventilate. Sweat was pouring down my face and into my blouse. I looked at the officer and said, "You don't have to remove me because I am leaving," and then I ran from the hospital. I have never been one to run, but I ran that day and I did not stop until I reached the motel. I ran up the stairs and down the corridor to my room. I tried to get the key into the lock, but my hands were shaking too much. On the third try, I was able to open the door and I got inside before I crashed. All of the years of pain hit me at once. I fell across the bed and my body convulsed with pain. All I could hear over and over was *"Your son is dying and the process has already started."* I felt as if I had been given surgery without anesthesia. I felt as though my heart had been cut out of my chest without the benefit of pain medication. I felt like I was dying *too* and the process had just started. I cried out over and over and over, "Oh, God, no, no, nooooooooo." I was on the floor, balled up in the fetal position, rocking back and forth, praying to God, *"Take me, take me, oh, God, take me, but please don't take my child!"*

CHAPTER TWENTY-FOUR

Somewhere in the back of my mind I heard the telephone ringing. It sounded like it was far away. I could hear the ringing sound, but I did not know where it was coming from. When I realized that the phone was not going to stop ringing unless I picked it up, I crawled from my spot on the floor over to the nightstand so that I could reach it. I picked it up and was barely able to utter a hello sound. It was my daughter, Peanut, and she had called to ask how Isidro was, but I guess the sound of my voice gave her the answer. She asked in an apprehensive voice, "What happened, Ma?"

The sound of her voice made me burst out in tears again. As hard as it was for me to hear it, it was going to be harder to tell her that her oldest brother, the one she was so close to that they were almost like twins, was dying. I decided to use the direct approach like the doctor did and just come out with it, although I know that in her heart she knew from the sound of my voice what I was going to say. This is what happens when people are connected. I said, "Peanut, he is dying! The doctor said that he is dying and the process has already started."

She screamed, "Oh, no!" and then burst out crying.

I kept calling her name, but she did not answer. Someone

in her office came and took the phone from her hand and told me that they were going to try to calm her down. I said, "Thank you," and then hung up the phone.

I got ready for the next call. Each time I received a call I would have to tell a friend or family member that my son was dying and each time I did, I would hear that doctor's words over and over again in my mind. *"Your son is dying and the process has already started."* This was something that I was going to have to do several times over the next couple of days. I had to tell my family members that my son was going to die.

I guess I slipped into a catatonic state because I walked around like a zombie for the next couple of hours. I would go to the hospital and sit by my son's bedside and just stare at him. I did not want the guards to see me cry, so when I could not hold back the tears, I would get up and walk out of the room. Sometimes I would walk across the street and buy scratch tickets and then walk around scratching them. Most of the time, I would go down to the chapel to pray. At times I did not even know what to pray for. *Was I asking God to keep my son alive so that he could spend another fifteen years in prison? Would he rather die than to spend that much more time in jail?* I did not have any answers, but I just kept praying and praying. I kept saying, *"God, help me. God, help my son. God, help my child."* When I would get to the point that I could stop crying, I would go back to my son's room and sit by his bedside again. It was at one of these times that a woman came into the room and introduced herself as a clergy intern for the Mayo Clinic. I did not even think of asking her who sent her or why she was there. I was just grateful to have someone to talk to. I could not talk to the nurses. I had been forbidden to speak to the doctors and I did not want to talk to the guards. It is sad, but as nice as this lady was to me, I cannot remember her name although I promised her that I would keep in touch with her. I hope she understands what my state of mind was like during that time and finds it in her heart to forgive me for not keeping my word.

Sometimes I don't think I would have made it through the days without her. She was the only person that the prison guards did not harass and it was very comforting to have her there with me. She would sit by Isidro's bedside and pray with me. One time I couldn't control myself and burst out in tears. She took me by the arm and led me to a waiting area and then went and got some tissues for me. She sat down beside me and told me that she thought that I was very brave because she had two sons and she knew she would not be able to stand it if someone told her that one of them were going to die. She started asking me questions about where I was staying in town and the conversation somehow got to the subject of the prison officials. I told her how they were making it so hard for me and she asked me to explain this. I went on to tell her how they had made me go all the way to the prison just to sign a form before I could get into the hospital to see my son.

She said, "They can't do that, it's not right."

I said, "Yes, they can. They can do anything they want."

She said, "Oh, yeah, well, we will see about that!"

She meant what she said too because that night I got a call from an official at the Bureau of Prisons who said that I would not have to go to the prison to fill out the form any more. I was very grateful for this because it was very expensive to go back and forth to the prison just to fill out a form when my son was a block and a half away from the motel. We sat and talked a little while longer and then I asked her to do a favor for me and pray the rosary with me. She made arrangements for a nun to accompany us to the chapel to pray the rosary and I was glad, although the nun was not very friendly and seemed in a hurry to get back to whatever it was that she was doing. After we prayed the rosary, we went back up to Isidro's room to sit by his bedside again.

The clergy intern and I were sitting at Isidro's bedside when a nurse came in to give him his medications. She was very attentive to Isidro and seemed truly concerned with his care. She handled him as if he was a newborn baby and she always made sure he was clean and comfortable. She would talk to Isidro as if he was going to answer her back and this made me feel good because for the first time in years someone, other than myself and other family members, was treating Isidro like he was a person again. She straightened up his bed, fluffed up his pillows and announced that she would be right back with his medications. When she came back, she had a cup full of pills and a cup of water. She held his head up and put the pills in his mouth and then gave him some water. Being a mother, I noticed that one of the pills was still in his mouth and I told her that I did not think that he had swallowed it. She said she thought he did, but when I opened his mouth, we could see that the pill was still there. I asked her if she could get some cranberry juice for me and she said yes and went off to find the juice. The clergy intern asked me if cranberry juice was his favorite and I said yes. Actually, I did not even know if Isidro liked cranberry juice, but I had read somewhere that cranberry juice was like an antibiotic and I somehow felt that if I could get my son to drink some cranberry juice, it would help him.

The nurse came back and announced that she did not have cranberry juice, but she did have some apple juice. I asked if I could go downstairs and buy some cranberry juice for him and was not surprised when I was told no. I took that apple juice from the nurse, thanked her, moved over to Isidro's bed, lifted him up and placed my left hand on the back of his head while holding the juice in my right hand. I said very softly, "Isidro, Isidro." His eyelids fluttered a little. He opened them and looked at me for the first time since I had arrived in Minnesota. I said, "Isidro, drink the juice so that you can swallow the pill, son." He blinked a couple more times and then began to sip the juice that I had put to his lips. He swallowed a couple of sips of the juice and then closed his eyes again. I called him again and he blinked some more, took a couple more sips of the juice and then closed his eyes back again. His responding made me immensely happy. I had not given up on him and in my mind, miracles do happen.

After I straightened out his sheets, I had to go back outside of the room because my tears had started to fall again. When he opened his eyes after blinking a few times, he looked so much like he did on the day he was born. I remember that day like it was yesterday. When they handed him to me, he had his eyes closed, but when I placed my finger in his tiny little hand, he grabbed it and held on tight. He also blinked a couple of times just like he had done a few minutes ago. We were in another hospital, in another time and place, so long ago. When he blinked on that first day, my heart was so full of joy, but when he blinked in that room a few minutes ago, it filled my heart with pain and sadness. I had to get outside to get some air because my chest was closing in on me again. The clergy intern followed me outside like she was afraid of what I might do and honestly, I was glad because I don't know what I would have done without her during those times.

We walked around talking for a while and then we headed back to the hospital. I stopped by to see Isidro and instead of sitting down, I went back to the chapel again. Being in the chapel gave me a sort of peace that I did not have while sitting in that room. It was there that the clergy intern suggested that we get a priest to give Isidro his last rites. I was glad that she mentioned it because it was something that I had not thought of. At the same time, it sort of made things kind of final and I was not quite ready to accept the fact that my son's life was really coming to an end. Hearing that he was dying was one thing, but giving him his last rites was making it a reality that I was not ready for.

In my mind, there was a miracle going to happen to make Isidro healthy again. *My* God, the God that I had always believed in, was not going to let my son die. I stayed in the chapel for a while and the intern went to make arrangements for the priest to come to Isidro's bedside. I went back to the room and just stood at the bedside watching Isidro. Every once in a while, his eyelids would flutter as they normally did when he was asleep.

When the priest came into the room with the intern, I immediately began to cry. I did not want the priest to talk too loud because I was afraid that Isidro would wake up and realize that he was being given his last rites and it would scare him. I voiced my concerns to the intern before the priest began the rites and she said she understood and told the priest what I had said. I was crying uncontrollably as the priest began his rites. It started to hit me again, *my son was dying and the process had already started.*

The intern came around to the side of the bed that I was on and put her arms around me. Before long she was crying as hard as I was. I started to feel real cold and my body began to shake. My knees felt weak and my head began to spin. At that moment, I wanted to die too. I could not stand the fact that my son was dying and that he was going to die without waking up so that I could tell him I loved him one more time. The priest finished giving Isidro his last rites and asked me if I wanted to take Holy Communion and I said yes. I felt that it was the right thing to do, but at that moment, I was kind of mad with God. I kept asking myself why did

Isidro have to suffer for seven-and-a-half long years only to die in custody. I sat down in the chair by Isidro's bedside and just let the tears flow. This time I did not care about the guards, or anyone else, coming into the room. The only thing that I cared about was my son lying in that bed, knowing that he was never going to get up again. All I cared about was that my son had spent all that time in prison only to die alone and so far away from home. I thought about all of the times that I had begged the prison officials to give my son a proper physical because I could see that he did not look well. All I cared about was that my son was dying and there was nothing I could do about it. I knew in my heart that if my son had been home and sick that I could have taken care of him and made him well. No one could tell me different.

As I sat there crying and rocking back and forth, I began to wonder what my son had been thinking and feeling lately. *Did he know that something was terribly wrong? Did he keep silent about this because he would rather be dead than spend fifteen more years in jail. Did he not tell me anything because he did not want to see me cry, thereby making it harder for him? Was he afraid?* The more I thought, the worse I felt, not for myself but for my son. For my entire life, whenever something bad happened, I would concentrate on something good to keep from feeling bad. At that moment, I began to think of how Isidro always had a way of getting out of doing things that he did not want to do or that he did not feel was right. I focused on the fact that Isidro was not going to do no damn twenty-three years in prison. He was getting out early. He was not getting out the way I wanted him out, but he was getting out. *My son was going to be free! My son was going to a place where no one could ever hurt him or lock him up again.* Fuck the Feds! *My son was getting out of prison!* With that thought, I stopped crying and I told the clergy intern that I was feeling a little better.

She stayed with me for a while longer and then said that she had to be getting home, but she would see me the next day. She gave me a big hug and then left the room. I had a feeling that she should have gotten off work hours ago because she was there at 8 o'clock in the morning and it was nearly 8 o'clock in the evening, time for visiting hours to end. I just sat there and acted like I did not know what time it was because I was not ready to leave yet. The guards must have sensed something in my demeanor because for once, they did not harass or bother me, but just allowed me to sit there.

Not long after the clergy intern left, another woman came in and introduced herself to me as Sister Emily Borman from the Federal Medical Center. She said that she was the chaplain of the prison. She sat down with me for a short time and then she said that it was well past visiting hours and that we should be leaving so that we would not have any trouble with the hospital staff. We walked to the hospital elevator and rode down in silence. When we got to the hospital lobby, Sister Emily asked me when the last time I had eaten anything was. Trying to avoid a long speech about having to eat something, I lied and said, "This morning."

She quickly asked me what I ate and I was too slow in thinking and said, "I forgot."

She smiled and suggested we walk across the street to the diner. I was not in the mood to protest so I just went along. Looking back, I can see what my state of mind was. I ordered a cheeseburger deluxe. Anyone who knows me knows that I hate hamburgers. I guess it comes from the flashbacks I get when I think about the hamburgers that my mother used to make. They were so dry and hard that they could be used for weapons. Anyway, I ordered a cheeseburger deluxe so that I would not have to bother reading the menu because I knew that whatever I ordered I was not going to eat.

While we were waiting for the food, we started discussing my son. I told her about him as a young child and as a young adult. I told her about our family and his children and how not having him around was going to affect their lives. We talked and talked until the cheeseburger deluxe was ready and then we got up to leave. Sister Emily offered to walk back to the motel with me and I immediately said okay because I was glad for the company. I knew that I had an important decision to make that night and I wanted to delay it for as long as I could. I don't remember everything we talked about, but I do remember telling her that my son did not have insurance and that I would need money to bury him. I spoke about getting back to work so that I could make that money because it would kill me if I could not give my son a proper funeral and burial. She told me that the Bureau of Prisons would put him in a mid-range casket and that they would provide a suit in which to bury him. It was too much for me, discussing my son's funeral, and I burst out in tears again. I told her that I did not want my son to die alone and far away from home. I told her that I did not want to leave him there, so many miles away from home and the people who loved him so much. It was then that she promised me that she would not let him die alone. It's funny how we make promises that we mean to keep, but things just don't work out the way we plan them.

When we got back to the motel, Sister Emily insisted that I eat the food that I had purchased. I opened the food and started to pick at the French fries while trying to find an excuse not to eat the hamburger. I nibbled at the pickle in silence as Sister Emily sat across from me giving me a look that said that she was not going anywhere until I ate at least some of the food. I tried eating the French fries, but they tasted like paste in my mouth, and I began to feel afraid that if I ate too many of them that my mouth would be permanently glued shut. I just sat there nibbling at the food and wishing that she would leave so that I could smoke a cigarette. I wanted her to leave and at the same time, I wanted her to stay because I was afraid of being alone. I think Sister Emily felt the same way as I did. She probably wanted to leave but felt uncomfortable about leaving me alone. We sat for quite some time. Sister Emily asked about my family and how they were holding up with all that was going on. I began to tell her about my children and grandchildren and at some point I began to talk about Isidro's life. At first it was easy to talk about Isidro, but when his present condition crept into my mind, I just lapsed into silence. Sister Emily just sat by quietly and left me with my private thoughts about my son. After some time went by, Sister Emily said that she had to leave and that she would see me sometime the next day. I said okay and gratefully accepted the big hug that she gave me and walked her to the door, knowing that if I followed my secret plan, that I would never, ever see her again in my life.

As soon as I felt that Sister Emily was out of sight, I ran back into the room and got out my cigarettes. Since the room was a no-smoking room, I had to go outside. I stepped out onto the balcony and took a long, deep drag of my cigarette. After enjoying a few drags of the cigarette, I began to get that *closed in* feeling again. From the time I arrived in Minnesota, every time I was alone for a few minutes I would get that *closed in* feeling, like I could not get enough air. I decided to take a walk across the street to the Super A gas station and purchase a few scratch tickets. The fresh air and the walk would do me good and the scratch tickets would give me a few seconds of escape from reality. I had made so many trips back and forth to the Super A that the night clerk recognized my face when I came in. He became very friendly after seeing my face several times the first night that I was in Minnesota and asked me about my visit there. I told him about my son and his condition and each time I came in, he would ask me if I'd just come from the hospital and then he would ask how my son was doing. I guess something about the look on my face that night kept him from asking how Isidro was. I guess the expression on my face said it all. I suppose that working in a location so close to the Mayo Clinic, he had come in contact with families whose loved ones were not doing well and he had come to know the look of pain on the faces of the people with whom he came in contact. He gave me a slight friendly smile but avoided looking directly at me. I was very grateful for this small act of kindness because any mention of my son at that moment would have caused a flood of tears that I had been holding back all evening. I took my purchase and my scratch tickets and began the journey back to my hotel room feeling like my shoes were lined with lead. Putting one foot in front of the other had become increasingly harder with each step I took in the state of Minnesota.

CHAPTER TWENTY-FIVE

I walked back to the motel while smoking cigarettes and scratching lottery tickets. Each time I scratched a winning ticket, I turned around and went back to the Super A to cash it in and purchase another ticket, which was my way of putting off going back to that lonely motel room by myself and thereby delaying the pain and tears that I knew were going to come as soon as I closed that motel room door. Each time I would get close to the motel entrance, I would win two dollars, five dollars, and one time a whopping forty dollars. On one of the trips from the Super A, I noticed a blue van that had been driving back and forth as I had been walking. This time the driver pulled up along side me and asked me how much. At first I thought he was asking me how much I had won, and then it dawned on me that he had seen me walking back and forth in close proximity to the motel and probably thought I was a hooker. That thought made me laugh! Here I was, over half a hundred years old and this guy thought I was a street walker. I laughed out loud and told him that if he tried that shit in New York City, he would have been taken around the corner and robbed. I then decided to get back to the motel before something else happened to make my life more miserable than it already was, as if that was possible.

I puffed my last cigarette and headed toward the stairs that would take me back to my room. When I got to the top of the stairs, I turned around and saw the blue van make a U-turn and head slowly toward the side of the motel driveway. I hurried inside, locked the door and put the chain on. For a moment I thought of dragging the dresser across the floor and placing it behind the door. That was before I realized that the dresser was bolted to the floor. My second thought was that I did not even need to lock the door because I had so much rage built up inside of me that if anyone had come through that door, they would have surely caught something that was not intended for them. I lay across the bed and waited for the thoughts that I had been avoiding for hours to come, unwanted, into my head. It was going to be another long night.

CHAPTER TWENTY-SIX

I took my clothes off and placed them on the chair next to the bed and then turned on the TV set. There was nothing on that interested me so I tuned into the nightly news to see what was going on in the state of Minnesota and in the city of Rochester. It was a while before I realized that I had not heard a word that the commentator had said. My thoughts were on my son. *What was I going to do?* He had no insurance and I had no money but I had to give my child a decent funeral. If I left to go back to New York and back to work, then I would have to leave him alone and at the mercy of the Bureau of Prisons. *If I stayed and waited for him to die, then how would I bury him?* I did not want my child to die alone with no one who loved him at his side. *Would they take care of him until the end?* He seemed so thirsty. *Would they raise his head and give him a cool glass of water or juice to drink or would they just let him lie there and wait for him to take his last breath? Why was this happening to me? What had I done so wrong that I was being punished this way? Was God angry with me?* The tears began to flow and a picture of my first-born child lying in that hospital bed flashed across my mind. *If I stayed until the end, then how would I get the money to bury him when the time came?* I thought of my brother-in-law, Willie, who had died a few years before. He too had no insurance and had passed away. I could remember sitting at his funeral, looking at him lying in the casket and thinking that now I knew the true meaning of the term *"pine box"* because what he was lying in was surely not a real casket. Thank God for my daughter's Navy pay or there would have been little or no flowers either. No, there was no way I was going to put my son away like that, I didn't care what I had to do, but he was going to have a decent funeral.

Just then the phone rang. It was my friend, Trellis, from work, calling to see how Isidro was doing and how I was holding up. I was glad to hear from Trellis because I knew that she, if anyone, knew what I was going through and what I was feeling. Trellis had just lost her daughter, her first-born, Amber, just the year before. When I told her that it was just a matter of time, she started asking questions. I told her what the doctors told me and explained to her that I did not think that Isidro knew I was there. She gave me some advice that I am grateful for to this day. She said, "Teresa, if he don't know that you are there, then you need to come back to work to make some money so that you can pay for his funeral." She also said, "I know it is going to be hard to leave him, but that's what you have to do." She went on to tell me about Amber's last days. She even told me how she held Amber in her arms until she took her last breath.

I knew I was not that strong. Amber had been born with cerebral palsy and I had always admired Trellis for the way she took care of her child, especially because she had been so young when Amber was born. When most girls her age were going out socializing and partying, Trellis was home taking very good care of Amber. I spoke to Trellis for a while longer and told her I was tired and that I would call her the following day. We said our goodbyes and then we both hung up. I got on my knees with my hands clasped together and prayed. I asked God to give me the strength to do what I had to do and to get my family and me through this. I knew it was going to be hard. I had no idea how I was going to make it. I figured I would just bug out, lose my mind and then everything would be okay because I would be crazy and not know what was happening. I said, yes, that's it, God, let me go crazy and then I won't suffer.

I stayed on my knees praying for God to help us until they began to hurt. I got up and went to the bathroom and let the water run. There is something soothing about the sound of running water. I got out my toilet items, got into the shower and let the water run down my aching body from head to toe. Unlike most black folk, I did not worry about my hair. I just let the water run until it began to get cold. I guess the small town motels only keep a small supply of hot water, which was a good thing that night. I got out of the shower, dried off with the rough motel towel, gave myself a deep lotion rub, put on my nightgown and got into bed. I was always afraid of the dark, but for some reason, I turned out the light that night. It was then and there that I decided what I was going to do. I was going to get up in the morning, go to the hospital, say goodbye to my son and head home for whatever lay ahead of me. God had given me a plan, but the hard part was going to be carrying it out. I fell asleep with deep sobs wracking my body.

CHAPTER TWENTY-SEVEN

I don't know how long I had been asleep when the sunlight, blaring through the windows, woke me up. I took a long, deep breath to try to prepare myself mentally for the day ahead of me. Before my feet touched the floor, the phone on the bedside table rang. It was a representative from the Bureau of Prisons. He stated that he had a form that he needed me to sign. I was really annoyed because I barely had time to gather my thoughts for the day before they started harassing me with their bullshit. Signing forms for the Bureau of Prisons was not a part of my game plan for the day. Besides, any form that they wanted me to sign was surely for their benefit and not that of Isidro or for me. He could take his form and shove it where the sun didn't shine for all I cared. I had much more important things to think about. Whenever I have something serious on my mind, I seem to have difficulty breathing and this morning was not different. I was fighting back tears, I could hardly breathe, yet I had to keep it moving. I took my time showering and dressing, but what I really wanted to do was to get back into bed, cover up my head and sleep, something I had not done for a long time. In fact, it had been years since I had a good night's sleep. In fact, the last time I had a full night of sleep was the night before my son was arrested.

I gathered all of my belongings and packed my bag since I would not be returning to the room. I then picked up the phone and called the van service that would take me to the airport and made a reservation. The van driver would pick me up in front of the hospital in exactly one hour. When I was ready to go, I gave the room a once over and went downstairs to settle my bill. The desk clerk seemed bright and chipper and it was all I could do to keep from asking her what the hell she had to be so happy about. All I wanted to do was pay my bill and be on my miserable way. After what seemed like an eternity, I was finally given my receipt and I stepped out into the street, blinded by the sun. I wondered if there was anyone else in the world as unhappy as I was on such a beautiful day. As I headed toward the hospital, I looked down and was amazed at how clean the streets were. *How could such a busy place be kept so clean?* I walked in a daze looking for so much as a cigarette butt, which I did not see. Too soon, I was at the hospital and I wondered what kind of crap the feds were going to put me through that morning. They had told me not to bring my pocketbook to the hospital and here I was with my pocketbook and suitcase too. I was moving with a purpose and they were not going to deter me. I got on the elevator with a bunch of strangers who had no idea of the amount of pain that I was in. Nurses with their crisp white uniforms, the kind you don't see in New York hospitals anymore. Doctors so deep in medical conversation that they did not even realize that other people were in the elevator discussing patient conditions like one would discuss the weather forecast. They were all oblivious to the black woman riding in their midst whose heart was broken in a million pieces. They could fix a lot of things, but they could not repair my broken heart.

When I reached my floor, I began to fight back the tears. Just in case my son *did* see or recognize me, I did not want him to see me crying. I had to be strong for Isidro. As I entered the room, the correction officers looked at me with my bags and I guess they figured that I was leaving because they did not make any of their usual smart remarks. As they had done each time I entered the room, the female officer called someone on the phone and told them that I was there. I could tell that whoever she was talking with let her know that they were on the way with the form that they wanted me to sign. I am sure that they knew from the look in my eyes that it would be better to let me leave without a scene. I could not have been feeling that much pain without some of it showing in my eyes or on my face.

I placed my bags on the floor near the entrance to the room and went over to my son's bed. I looked at him and was so happy that he was clean and looked very comfortable. I could see that he had recently received his morning care and this gave me some sense of comfort knowing that someone there cared. It did not matter if they were doing it because I was there or not, just as long as it had been done. I took my son's hand in mine and began to stroke it lightly. I was afraid to speak because I did not want my voice to start breaking up nor did I want the officers to hear what would be my last words to my son. I just sat there holding his hand for a moment. I thought of one of the many jokes that Isidro had told me through the years. It was something about burying him upside down so that the world could kiss his ass. I wanted to say, *"Son, let me turn you over right now so that these officers here can be the first to kiss your ass,"* but I knew that they would not take kindly to this so I did not say it but I was surely thinking it. I sat there rubbing his hands, wishing that I could just take him by the hand, lead him out of the hospital and take him home with me. My son was lying there as if he were sleeping peacefully. It reminded me so much of the day when he was born when I stood in front of the nursery, proudly staring down at my first-born child. We had both come a long way since that first joyful day. His body was now warm to the touch and then I thought that the next time I would see him that he would be cold and no longer breathing. His heart would no longer be beating. I could not hold back the tears. I took my son's hand and said, "Isidro, I always thought that you were mine, but I now know that you belong to God. God just lent you to me for a while and he is taking you back now. I love you, son." As I was saying this, the two officers stood up and stepped out of the room. I grabbed my son for one last time and held him close to me. I whispered to him that I loved him and that I would see him when I got home. I turned around, picked up my bags and fled the room.

I ran down the corridor blinded by tears and hardly able to breath. As I was fleeing, I passed two men dressed in suits and I overheard one say, "We have to get her to sign the form before she leaves."

I felt like the world was closing in on me and that I was going to pass out, so when I saw a ladies room, I ran inside. I put my bags on the floor and held onto the sink. My chest was heaving up and down as I leaned over the basin to splash some cold water on my face. As I did this, I glanced down at my watch. I had ten minutes to get to the van, so I quickly wiped my face with some rough paper towels, grabbed my luggage and headed for the elevator. It was then that I saw the two men walking excitedly down the hall glancing from room to room, one with some papers in his hand. It was obvious that they were looking for me. Had they just bothered to turn around and look back, they would have seen me, but they didn't. I got on the elevator, took it to the first floor and headed for the front lobby of the hospital. I could

see the van waiting outside. When the driver saw me running toward the van, he got out and walked around the van
to take my things. I got into the van and waited while the
driver packed my bags in the rear of the van. I did not dare
look at the hospital because I was afraid that if I did I would
jump from the van and run back upstairs to my son's room.
The driver got back into the van and pulled off. It wasn't
until we were a safe distance away that I glanced back and
took my final look at the *Mayo Clinic*. It was such a bright
shiny day, but I felt like I was in the black hole of hell.

I can vaguely remember the picturesque view of the countryside with its many lakes as we drove toward the airport. I
can also remember getting to the counter and being told
that my flight was not for another five hours. I can remember asking the agent to get me on any flight leaving
Minnesota that was heading in the general direction of New
York. I was told that I could get a flight to Philadelphia that
would give me a connection to New York and that the flight
was leaving soon, but if I hurried up, I could catch it. I quickly
said that I would take the flight knowing that if I did not get
out of Minnesota immediately, I would never leave. If I did
not leave right away, I would turn around and go back to
the Mayo Clinic to wait for my son to die. I could not do
this, I was not that strong.

Somehow I made my way to the plane where I was seated
next to a very nice elderly white man. Shortly into the flight,
I noticed that the gentleman was crying quietly. I asked him
if he was okay and he began to tell me how he had come to
Minnesota to get a prosthetic leg and that it was not fitted
properly and was very painful. He said that he had noticed
me crying too and asked what was wrong and I told him.
He was very sympathetic and said that I had made him feel
foolish. When I asked why, he said that all he had to do
about his problem was remove the leg, but there was noth-

ing that I could do about my problem. This did not make me feel any better, but it was comforting to know that someone cared. We both chatted for a while and before long, the plane landed in Philadelphia. I wished him well and we parted at the gate. To this day I wonder whatever happened to this very kind old man.

CHAPTER TWENTY-EIGHT

had three hours to kill before my flight for New York departed, so I decided to find a phone and call my cousins, Reggie and Yolanda, who lived in Philadelphia. I spoke to them and they said that they would see what they could do about coming there to meet me. I then walked around thinking that I should get something to eat because by then it was after three in the afternoon and I had not had anything all that day. I walked around the food court, but could not bring myself to anything that looked like I could eat it. Besides, the food court was full of noisy children with happy parents and every male I saw made me angry that my son was dying and all of these people were still alive *AND* happy. I wandered around until I found a bar and grill. I knew that I shouldn't drink without eating, but at that point I did not care. I sat down and ordered a vodka and cranberry juice. I must have been on my third one when all of a sudden my cousin Yolanda came into the bar. I was so happy to see her that I jumped off of the bar stool and went running toward her. She pulled me into her arms and held me tight. The dam of tears burst again. We stood there embracing for a few minutes and then we both sat down at the bar. This was probably the first time in her life that Yolanda ever took a seat on a barstool. She is the real religious type and being in a bar was not her cup of tea and I knew this. So, instead of sitting there and having a few more drinks, I decided to walk around and talk to Yolanda while waiting for the plane. She took my hand and we strolled around the airport talking about my trip to Minnesota and what was happening to Isidro. I explained to her what the doctors said and what to expect. She continued to hold my hand and said, "Just pray and trust in God."

I seemed to draw strength from her belief in the Almighty because up to that point I had lost all faith and could not understand why this was happening to me, to my son *and* to my family.

When I was alone, the time was creeping by, but since Yolanda came, it seemed like the time was flying by and before long it was time for me to board the plane for the last leg of my journey. Although I wanted to get home where I would be surrounded by loved ones, I was in no hurry to tell the family that our precious son, brother and father was going to die. I could still hear those words echoing in my head, *"Ma'am, your son is dying and the process has already started."* Just the thought of those words again brought tears to my eyes. I needed to be strong so I could help the rest of my family. We had all suffered so much since Isidro had been incarcerated and now we were going to feel the ultimate pain. Every time I thought of my first-born child dying, alone and far away from home, and the many people who loved him so much, I wanted to die too. At least if he were closer to home, we could all take turns spending time with him. Again, I got that feeling of turning around and going back to Minnesota to stay with my son till the end. Then the picture of a pine box crept into my head and I felt that I was doing the right thing.

Yolanda and I hugged and kissed goodbye and I headed down the ramp and onto the plane. I could not look back because I was afraid that I would see Yolanda crying and I would fall apart again too. It had been only two weeks since Yolanda had buried her mother and a year since she buried her father. I could remember sitting in church at my Aunt Eloise's funeral and wondering where Yolanda and her younger brother Michael had gotten the strength. I would soon find out.

I took my assigned seat and looked out of the window as the plane began to ascend. When we began to reach the clouds in the sky, I started to think about death and what it meant. *Was there a life hereafter? Would my son go to heaven? Would he be able to see me from heaven? Would he know when he passed away, how much we loved him? Was he afraid? Was he hungry or thirsty?* Each time a new set of questions came into my head I would try to change my thoughts because they were just too painful to think about. I sat on the plane trying to read the newspaper and magazines, but I just could not concentrate on anything. My thoughts kept going back to my precious son, lying in that hospital sick and alone. The truth, which I found out later, would have been too painful for me to bear.

The plane landed and I somehow made my way to the passenger pick up area. My daughter had made arrangements for a family friend to pick me up when my plane arrived. He was not there, so I called home to see if anyone knew what was going on. My daughter, Peanut, sounded very annoyed on learning that I was standing in the airport alone. She said that she wanted him to be there so I did not have to spend any time alone, but I guess he got caught in traffic or either he was just on BPT (Black People's Time).

Just as I was beginning to feel anxious and annoyed, my friend Paul pulled up at the airport pick up stand in front of a yellow cab. I hurried to the car so I could have a cigarette and a seat, in that order. I guess Paul had heard the news about Isidro because he did not ask any questions about him, but instead asked how I was feeling. I just shook my head and said okay because I did not feel that I could talk without crying yet and I knew that I had lots of that to come. We took the expressway heading toward the Bronx and I sat back in silence, wondering where I was going to get the strength to face my other children with the news of Isidro's impending death. We got to the Whitestone Bridge in no time and too soon, we were pulling up in front of my house on Rhinelander Avenue. I got out of the car and stood on the sidewalk while I waited for Paul to get my bag out of the trunk of the car. He had the car door open and I was listening to the song by Janet Jackson, *Control*. It reminded me of how much Isidro loved Janet Jackson. He would look at her videos and listen to her songs for hours. He thought she was the most beautiful woman in the world. I had to walk away from the car because that song, like everything else, was beginning to make me cry. I walked into the lobby, pressed for the elevator and waited for Paul out of earshot of the car stereo. I could not afford to cry just then. The time for tears was coming, and coming fast.

I opened the door, stepped into the house and found everyone just as I expected. They were all there, sitting in the living room, waiting for the news about Isidro. I put my bag down by the kitchen door and went into the kitchen, pretending to be thirsty. I had used every stall tactic that I could come up with and now there was no more putting it off. I had to tell my children that their brother was dying. No matter what words I used, the outcome would still be the same. There was no way for me to soften the blow, so I just sat down and came out with it. I told them exactly what the doctor in the Mayo Clinic had told me, that Isidro was dying, that the process had already started and that there was no way to predict how much longer he would live. As expected, everyone began to scream and cry, except Ricky, the baby brother. As soon as they began to cry, I began to cry too. Ricky just stood there looking like he felt very sorry for us all but that he did not know what to do. I will never forget the look on his face that night. There was a look of pain but at the same time, there was determination in those young eyes. Years later, when I would look back on that day, I think Ricky was saying to himself that he would take care of all of us and that he would never do anything that would cause any of us the pain that he saw that day.

We all cried together with Ricky standing by looking lost and helpless. As I had begun to do in the past few weeks and months, I caught my breath and willed myself to get a grip on things and pull myself together. I told my daughters that Isidro would not want to see us crying. They all knew that Isidro never liked to see anyone cry. Peanut jumped up and said, "He sure wouldn't," and seemed to instantly come together.

Sanyae was another matter. She continued to sob like she was never going to stop. I knew I had to do something quick so I began to yell at her. I said, "Look, crying is not going to get us anywhere. It is only going to make us sick and then we will not be able to do what we have to do." I guess something about the tone of my voice brought her out of it and she began to settle down a little.

We discussed what we were going to do about a funeral. I could not go to a funeral home and make arrangements for my son while he was still alive. Sanyae and Peanut decided that they would go to the funeral homes in the area the next morning and inquire about the prices. Although I was trying to put up a brave front for my children, inside I was dying. In my mind I kept asking why? *Why was this hap-*

pening to our family? We had always been good people so what could we have possibly done to deserve this? What could Isidro have done to deserve this? There were no answers, just pain and more pain.

Every time I thought of my son lying in that hospital bed, I felt like someone was driving an ice pick through my heart. I could not sit still. I would get up and walk to the kitchen. I would open the refrigerator and then close it without taking anything out. I made several trips to the bathroom to splash cold water on my face. Each time I spent more than a minute or two in the bathroom, one of my kids would knock on the door and ask if I was alright. I yelled out, "Yeah, I'm alright, can't I go to the bathroom in peace? I know y'all are worried about me, but I hope you're not going to start following me around like I am going to die too." That was not a nice thing for me to say, but it did get them away from the bathroom door, for a minute anyway. It was going to be a long night.

CHAPTER TWENTY-NINE

Bright and early the next morning, Sanyae and Peanut got up and went to the funeral home. Ricky went to school, I guess because he had nothing better to do and it would at least get him away from the crying for a while. I was beginning to get worried about Ricky because he was not showing any emotion at all and he was very close to his big brother. I asked him how he was feeling about everything and his answer to me was, "It's God's will." I wondered if he really felt this way or if he was saying that for my benefit. It brought me back to the time shortly after Isidro had been arrested when Ricky was standing around watching some kids ride their dirt bikes. Ricky came up to me and told me how much he wished that Isidro was home because he knew that he and Isidro would be riding bikes too. He walked away saying that he was going to ask them to give him a ride. I was sure that they would because they were some of the same kids that Isidro would ride with up and down the drive where we lived, when he was home. But I was wrong. The kids did not give Ricky a ride. They all knew Isidro was in prison so they did not have to be nice to his little brother anymore as he had once been to them. I was sitting there on the bench thinking that Ricky was riding and that he would be back soon when all of a sudden a guy came up to me and said, "Mrs. Teresa, Ricky is sitting on the ground crying."

When I asked him what happened, he said that he did not know. He said that he had asked Ricky what was wrong, but he did not want to say. I asked him to show me where Ricky was and he did. I walked up to him and said, "Ricky, what's wrong? Why are you crying?"

He just sat there with his little chest heaving up and down and when I asked him the second time, he said, "Mommy, I miss my brother. Nothing is the same since he left."

I felt so bad for him at that moment that I almost began to cry too. I put my arms around him and helped him to get up off of the ground. I said, "Don't worry, Ricky, Isidro will be home soon and then you will never have to ask these guys for anything, ever again." I said, "If they ask you or Isidro for a ride, you remind them how they treated you while Isidro was gone and make sure that he never gives them a ride again." Ricky broke out in a big fat Kool-Aid smile. I guess the thought of this happening gave him great pleasure and I was happy that he stopped crying. I may have made Ricky feel better then, but deep down inside, I wondered when, if ever, that Isidro would come home.

Before long, Peanut and Sanyae came back from the funeral homes and they were not too happy. Peanut said that both funeral homes said the same thing. They were told that if Isidro was still legally married, I would not be able to bury him, but that his wife would have to do this. I was consumed with rage. Now I was being told that I couldn't even bury my son. *What kind of shit was this?* I asked if they had explained that Isidro and his wife had not been together for over eight years and they said yes. I felt as if my life was spiraling out of control. Each new thing that happened made it worse and worse. *Was this ever going to end?* Again I asked myself, "*What did I do in life to deserve this?*

For some reason, Mrs. P came to my mind. It was she that started this whole mess in the first place. I was thinking that if she were alive, I would find her and kill her for what she had done to my son and my family. I immediately asked myself if I was being punished for the feelings that I had abut Mrs. P on the day that she had gotten killed. I had to shake my head a couple of times to make the thought go away. I did not have time for this. I had to think about getting my son buried. He was my son before he became a husband and it was my responsibility to bury him. There was no way that I was going to depend on anyone to bury my child. The nerve of them, *telling us that I could not bury my son.* I became full of rage. I was blinded by hatred. Hatred for Mrs. P, hatred for Debra Landis, the Assistant United States Attorney in my son's case, hatred for the judge who let this travesty of justice happen to us, and at that moment, I hated the entire world and almost everyone in it. I did not care what the funeral directors had to say about it. I just had to find a funeral home that would let me bury him. And, most importantly, I had to find the money.

Then I remembered the money that I had put in the bible. One of the police officers at my precinct had taken up a collection for me and had given it to me when I returned from Minnesota. My coworkers at the precinct knew that I had been taking off days and traveling back and forth to Rochester, Minnesota. I had taken off so many days that I was out of both vacation and sick time. They decided to take up a collection to help me out with my bills since I was in a *no pay* status. No one knew at the time that the money would not be used for a bill.

On the night that they had given it to me, I came home from work and placed it in the middle of my bible. I prayed to God to make it be enough for whatever I needed when the time came. It seemed as if the time was coming a little too fast for me. I went to the bible, took out the money and separated it into stacks of ones, fives, tens and twenties. When I finished counting, I had over two thousand dollars! I had no idea that it was so much. Immediately, I felt a huge burden lifted from my shoulders. With the two thousand and the money that I had in my bank and checking accounts, I would be able to bury my son. *Praise God.*

Somehow, I was able to get through the next few days and nights by putting one foot in front of the other. I was able to get on a bus and train and somehow make it to work. I was able to do my job, but later on down the road I found that I had made many, serious mistakes. My every waking moment was filled with thoughts of my precious son. As soon as I opened my eyes in the morning I would ask myself if this would be the day. I would wonder how he was doing and then I would get that feeling in the pit of my stomach. If I did not fight hard, the tears would begin to flow. I would wonder if he was clean and comfortable. I wondered if they had washed his face or his body. I thought of how he was left in his own waste and was being cared for by other inmates back in Pennsylvania. At least in Pennsylvania he had friends who knew him and cared about him. Now he was all the way in Minnesota where he knew no one and no one knew him or cared about him. I would see him sitting in the visiting room in that wheelchair and unable to even hold a cup for himself. I wondered if his lips were parched and dry and if he was in need of a cool drink. I thought about the night I could not sleep and got up at two in the morning and begged the prison officials to please give my son something to drink and make him cool, dry and comfortable in his hospital bed. I even asked the duty officer if he had any children and how would he feel if his child was dying alone and miles away from home. As hard as I tried when those thoughts filled my head, I could not help but cry. If I cried too much I would not be able to make it through the day. Some days when I cried too much early in the morning, I would lay back down after calling my job and just stay in the house and watch television. I would tune out the world by making believe that none of this was happening to Isidro and to our family. Sometimes this would work for a while. I would pretend that Isidro was still in Virginia working in his car shop and that Ricky would soon be home from school. I would pretend that when the weekend came, Ricky and I would take a trip to Virginia and relax for a couple of days. Some days I would go to the liquor store up the street, purchase a bottle of rum and then go home and try to drown my troubles away. Of course this only made things worse because with the liquor the tears were intensified. No matter what I did, my thoughts always came back to the reality that my first-born child was dying and that there was nothing that I could do to help him. The fact that I could not even be at his side was tearing my heart apart. I now wonder if God was sparing me the pain later on of having the memory of him taking his last breath.

CHAPTER THIRTY

When the sun was bright, I could always find a way to feel better about things. The sun shining reminded me of the day when my son was born. It also reminded me of him as a young boy who always wanted to be outside when it was sunny. I have fond memories of him sitting on the windowsill asking when the rain was going to stop so that he could go outside. We used to laugh and say that you could never tell the weather by Isidro because, according to him, if the sun was out, then it was hot outside. It seemed like the days before his death were bright and sunny. Looking back, I can only remember one day that was cloudy and that was the 4th of July 1998, nine days before Isidro's death. I remember that day so well because it was my fiftieth birthday and the most miserable day of my life up to that point. My family had planned a bus trip to the Maryland Harbor months earlier, but I could not bring myself to get on that bus because the last thing I felt like doing was celebrating anything. I had invited several coworkers and friends to join us on the trip, but at the last minute I called everyone and let them know not to expect me there. I told them that they had to go and have a good time, but that they would have to go without me.

They all understood and went along with my family to enjoy the day. I kept thinking that the day was just as gloomy and overcast as the day that Isidro was arrested. All of our family members and close friends knew that Isidro was close to death and I knew that they were hoping that Isidro did not pass away on my birthday. I knew that this was not going to happen because I knew my son. He had held on this long and he would hold on a little longer, but he would not die on my birthday. Not that it mattered because once he was gone I would never, ever again have a happy birthday or any happy day for that matter.

All of my children and a few friends had gathered at my house in hopes of brightening up my day a little, but all they did was get on my nerves. They kept asking me how I was feeling, did I want this or that, did I want to go somewhere, etc. I wanted to shout out that I did not want ANYTHING, that I felt like shit and that I did not want to go anywhere but to sleep where I could get away from my pain for a while. All of my grandchildren were there and they were looking forward to doing something for the 4th of July. I don't think that they grasped the concept that their father and uncle was going to die. The older ones knew what was going on, but I guess it was not a reality to them. Eventually, I let them talk me into going to Rye Playland Amusement Park. It was not so much that I wanted to go anywhere, but I needed to get some of those people out of my overcrowded house. We piled up in several cars and took 95 North to Rye, New York. It was a cloudy day and I was glad because the day seemed to fit my mood. None of the people at Rye Playland seemed to mind that there was no sun. There were hundreds of people walking around eating hot dogs, hamburgers and cotton candy. Children were begging their parents for just one more ride. Adults were walking around drinking soda or beer out of plastic cups while I walked around drowning in my misery. On one hand, I wanted to be out of the house, but on the other hand, I wanted to be near the phone in case the hospital called. Every time I thought of the hospital, my blood began to boil. When I was at the Mayo Clinic, I could see that Isidro was getting the best care, but the prison hospital was another matter. I was able to leave Isidro and return to New York because I was comfortable with the quality of care that he was receiving at the Mayo Clinic, but as soon as I left the hospital, Isidro was taken from the Mayo Clinic and put back in the prison hospital. When I found this out, I was infuriated. They had given me no indication that they were going to move my son. Had I known this I would have stayed with him and made sure that he was given the best care possible. The first time we went to visit Isidro in the prison hospital, we could see that he was both thirsty AND hungry. Those low down dirty bastards were doing everything in their power to make our family suffer along with Isidro. The only comforting thought that I had was that once Isidro passed away, they could never again do anything to hurt either him or any member of my family again. Or so I thought.

I don't know how long we stayed at Rye Playland, but soon, too soon, we were ready to go home again. We packed up the cars and headed southbound on I-95. During the day at Rye Playland I had been given several cups of mixed drinks. I did not know what the sweet liquid was nor did I care. All I knew was that every time someone handed me a cup and said *Happy Birthday*, I took it and gulped down the sweet liquid greedily. By the time we were ready to head for home, I was more than a little tipsy. This was a good thing because I went to sleep as soon as I got into the car. Before I knew anything, they were waking me up in front of my house. I really needed that alcohol-induced nap because it had been days since I'd actually slept. We went upstairs and spent the rest of the weekend eating and waiting for news about Isidro. The days were long, but the nights were longer. We tried to call to ask about his condition several times a day and most of the time we were put on hold for long periods of time. We were told to hold on and after holding on for ten to fifteen minutes, we would then hear a dial tone. Once I was even told by a Miss Jennifer Hoen that the staff and the Bureau of Prisons did not have time to be giving me a daily update on my son's condition and that if I wanted an update, I should call once, but not more than twice a week. I told her that I just wanted to make sure that my son was okay and that I was concerned if he was clean and being fed or at least being given fluids to drink. She then told me in no uncertain terms that my son was not being fed because he was in a coma. She went on to say that he was given IV fluids to keep him hydrated but that there was no way or no reason for him to be given foods. I wanted to *DIE. And,* at the same time I thought that if I could get my hands on this woman that I would kill her! I did not even get a chance to respond to her because when she finished saying what she had to say, she hung up the phone on me. *How could she be so cruel? Did she not have a mother or a grandmother?* This was the one and only time that I was glad that my son was far away because had there been any way that I could have gotten to that woman, the outcome would not have been good. I knew that my son was not doing well, but no one had ever told me that he was in a coma. *Was there no end to the heartlessness of these bastards?* As I had been doing quite frequently, I dropped to my knees and asked the Lord to take my hand and lead the way. Over and Over I asked why? *Why was God taking my son? Why could he not take me and let my precious baby live?* The questions went on and on but there were no answers.

I got up from my knees and went to the window to jerk the Venetian blinds shut. I did not want the brightness of the sun to come into my world. My inside world was dark and bleak and I wanted my outside world to be just as dark. I spent the next few days walking back and forth in a cloud of pain. Some days I even managed to get to work, although how I did is beyond me. I managed to cross the streets without looking for passing cars. I managed to get down into the subway and board a train that would take me to my destination without giving it a single thought. On the days that the sun shined the brightest, I was chilled to the bone and goose pimples covered my arms. People spoke to me and I answered without hearing what they had said. The days were hard, but the nights were harder. I would come home from work exhausted and go straight to bed only to wake up a couple of hours later and begin pacing the floor. I smoked one cigarette after another until I ran out and then I would get dressed and take my life in my hands by walking five blocks away to the 24-hour store, at three o'clock in the morning. Sometimes I would make several trips to the 24-hour store during the middle of the night to purchase scratch lottery tickets. I did anything that would take my mind off of my son lying in that prison hospital bed miles away from home and the many people who loved him. The minute I thought about him, the pain and the questions would come. *Is he hungry? Is he cold? Is he sleeping on clean sheets? Does he have a fever? Is he afraid? Does he call out for me or his dad during the middle of the night?* Then the tears would begin to flow. I would sob silently because I did not want to wake up Ricky who was sleeping in the next room. Some nights I could not control myself and I would wail to the top of my lungs.

Ricky would get up and try his best to comfort me. He would put his arm around my shoulder and say, "Don't cry, Ma, this is God's will."

I would wonder where he got his strength from. It would be years before he fell apart because of the loss of his brother.

CHAPTER THIRTY-ONE

A few days after learning that my son was in a coma, a sort of peace came over me and I accepted the fact that my son, my first-born child, was going to die. To ease the pain, I told myself that he would finally be out from behind those horrible prison walls. He would no longer be denied decent food and would not have to follow orders and suffer insults from those idiotic prison guards who would probably be working at cutting meat in the local supermarket had they not passed a civil service test and been given the job of high priced babysitters. And most important, I told myself that my son was going home to God who would wrap him in His arms where he could never be hurt, sick or locked up again. Once this peace came over me, I was able to sleep for a couple of hours straight each night, but I still did not have an appetite and could not remember the last time that I had eaten a real meal. At times I would start eating and then in the middle of the meal I would think about my son and lose my appetite. I would immediately begin to feel guilty, because here I was eating and my poor son had not had a decent meal in over seven years. I would push my plate away and try to concentrate on something that would take my mind off of food and then it would be days before I could force myself to eat again.

It was a Monday morning when I woke up and looked at the clock. It was 7:45 a.m. and I had overslept by fifteen minutes. Surprised that I had not only fallen into a deep sleep, only overslept, I jumped out of bed and headed for the shower. I had a strange feeling of well-being that I could not explain. I was standing under the stream of water which was massaging my body when I heard Ricky knocking on the bathroom door. I stuck my head through the shower curtain and asked him what he wanted. He said something I could not understand and I asked him to repeat it.

He yelled, "The phone, it sounds like one of your cop friends from the precinct."

I knew right away that it was not one of my friends because they all knew better than to call me at that time of the morning unless it was an emergency. Whoever it was, I knew it had to be important, so I hopped out of the shower, threw a large towel around me, opened the door and grabbed the phone from Ricky's hand. I said, "Hello" and got no answer. I said, "Hello" a few more times before shrugging my shoulders and hanging up. I got dressed and Ricky and I walked to the bus stop together. He did not have anywhere to go that morning and I thought it was nice of him to walk me to the bus stop. I waved goodbye to him as the bus pulled off and continued on my way to the train station alone.

When the train came in, I rushed to the corner seat, happy that I had snagged that lone seat in the corner of the train, because I knew that no one would be able to squeeze in next to me. I always judged the day ahead of me by the seat that I got on the train. If I got the lone corner seat, it would be the start of a great day. On the other hand, if I got squeezed into a seat in between two big people or next to someone that had music blaring out of a headset, or someone having a loud conversation on a cell phone, I would expect a stressful day ahead. In fact, I had even put together a train survival bag. The bag itself was to protect me from people who wanted to get too close. Headphone set to block out other folks' noise and conversations, a book to read and my rosary beads, which I had begun praying on a daily basis since my son took ill. The train was quiet so I took out my rosary beads and began to pray the rosary, oblivious to the people around me. Before long, I arrived at my destination and left the train to make the final leg of my journey, the elevator ride to the office. Happy to arrive on time without any major delays, I sat down and plunged into my work.

About 11 o'clock, the phone rang. For the last few weeks, every time the phone rang, I would get a sinking feeling in the pit of my stomach. This time was not different. I said, "Hello," and a male caller on the other end asked to speak to *Teresa Aviles*. I said this is she speaking. He identified himself as an official from the Bureau of Prisons. My heart sank and I said, "Yes," waiting to hear something that I really did not want to hear. He began telling me about a program that the Bureau of Prisons called the Compassionate Release Program which was offered to inmates who had less than one year to live. He went on to say that if I agreed to care for Isidro that he could possibly be sent home under this program. At first, apprehensive, I told him that I was not aware that Isidro had that long to live since he told me that the paperwork, which took approximately two to three weeks, would still have to be filed. I said, "Of course I am willing to care for him, he is my son." I was so excited that my heart began to race. I broke out in a sweat and I could hardly sit still as we continued our conversation. He ended the conversation by telling me that he would begin the paperwork and that I would hear from him very soon.

I hung up the phone and said, "Yes!" very loudly before

I remembered where I was. I stood up at my desk and began to pace around the office. Isidro was going to be sent home. God had answered his prayers and mine. I had to tell everyone. I sat back down and began to dial my daughter's work number. When she answered, I said, "Guess what?" I told her and she, like me, could not understand it. *Why and how were they going to send him home now?* I told her to just pray for him to hold on long enough to come home. I then called my younger daughter and my younger son and told them the same thing. Just pray for Isidro to hang on long enough to come home. In the end, Isidro was smarter than us all.

I was so happy. No longer was the sun shining in a dark place. My chills went away and for the first time in almost two months I was hungry. I made a few more calls to the family members that I could reach and told everyone the same thing, "Pray for Isidro to hold on until he got home." I then got up, took my pocketbook and went downstairs to get something to eat. I did not want to go too far away from the phone so I chose the Chinese buffet on the corner of Park Avenue and East 32nd Street. I was so hungry that I did not know what to pick out. I grabbed a plastic container and just began tossing things into it. Lettuce, tomatoes, cucumbers, chicken, beets, etc. It didn't really matter what I ate, but just that I finally had an appetite. I paid for my salad and left the restaurant as if I had wings on my feet. I thought about the feeling of well-being that I'd had since I woke up that morning and figured out that Isidro was the reason. Isidro was coming home, finally.

I went back to my office, washed my hands and sat down to enjoy my food. Although I was famished, I decided to take my time and savor every little morsel of food. I was just about to put the second forkful of food into my mouth when the phone rang. As I had been doing for the past couple of weeks, I answered it before the second ring. It was another official from the Bureau of Prisons. I did not catch his name but I knew it was not the same person that had called me less than an hour earlier. This person spoke much slower and hesitant like he was not sure exactly what it was that he had called for. He asked a second time if I was *Teresa Aviles* as if he had not heard me the first time. I said, a little louder this time, "Yes, this is *Teresa Aviles*. How can I help you?"

For a minute, he seemed to be searching for words, then he just blurted out, "Mrs. Aviles, I am sorry, but Isidro passed away this morning."

I dropped the phone, fell on my knees and let out a blood- curdling scream! I crossed my hands over my chest and held onto my arms and rocked back and forth screaming, "Noooo, nooooooooo, noooooooooo, not my baby."

A coworker, Betsy Radmore, came running in from the cubicle outside of my office. Betsy was one of the people who had been making phone calls to the Bureau of Prisons for me. As soon as she heard me scream, she came running and it was not necessary for her to ask me what had happened. She knew. She knew that I had just received the news that my precious first-born child had died. Somehow, Betsy was able to get me off of the floor and back into my chair. The phone rang again and it was my daughter, Sanyae. She asked if I was alright and I just said, "He's gone. Sanyae, Isidro is gone." She told me not to go anywhere, that she would be right there.

The phone rang again and it was Ricky. He said in barely a whisper, "Ma, Isidro died."

I said, "I know," and asked if he was okay. He said yes and then I told him that I would be on my way home. My supervisor, Nick, appeared from somewhere and very nervously asked how I was going to get home. I don't remember answering him, I just remember Betsy standing there with her arms around my shoulder, rubbing me lightly. I began to feel like the room was closing in on me, the air became very thick and the room began to spin. I mumbled something about going outside to get some air. What I really wanted to do was to go outside and fill my lungs with nicotine filled smoke. I knew before I left I would have to call my daughter, Peanut, to tell her the news. There was nothing to do but pick up the phone and tell her. There was no gentle way or no words to make it any easier. I picked up the phone and just said, "He's gone."

She said something like, "Oh, no, no, no," and then she too dropped the phone and began to wail.

I had to get out of my office, the walls were beginning to close in on me. I grabbed my pocketbook, knowing that I was not coming back anytime soon, and left the building with Betsy following close behind me. I will forever be thankful to Betsy for that five or ten minutes that she spent with me while I was waiting for Sanyae. I lit one cigarette and took a few long drags before dropping it on the ground and crushing it with the sole of my shoe only to light another one a few seconds later. Sanyae was there in a flash and I can remember feeling so glad that she was there because she was the strong sensible one. Sanyae thanked Betsy for being there for me and then she hailed a Yellow cab. We got in and headed for the Bronx. The two of us just sat in silence. I could not help but notice how bright and shiny the day was. Just like the day that Isidro was born. Sanyae was not crying or anything and kept looking at me out of the corner of her eye as if she was waiting for something to happen. Something was happening, but she was unable to see it from the outside. Inside, my heart was breaking into little pieces which were falling apart inside of my chest. Before we reached the Bronx, there was a huge hole in the place where my heart used to be. My first-born child had died. He was gone and there was no longer any hope of him ever coming home again. I wanted to die too. That is what Sanyae could not see. I wanted to lie down on the back seat of that cab and just die.

Before long, Sanyae was tapping me on my shoulder to let me know that we were in front of my building. I could not remember getting on the FDR Drive or crossing the 138th Street Bridge. All I could remember was getting into the cab and now we were in front of my house. We took the elevator to the fourth floor and somehow we got into my apartment. I don't know how we got inside because I do not remember taking out my keys or unlocking the door. Once inside, I did not know what to do. I did not know whether to sit or stand. I did not know if I was supposed to lie down or if I was supposed to walk around and cry. All I knew was that I was numb. I could hear a voice in my head telling me that Isidro, my son, had died. *Isidro died. Isidro died.* I kept hearing the words over and over and over. *God, tell me what to do next?* As if to answer my prayer, the phone rang. Sanyae answered it and I could hear her speaking softly into the phone although I could not understand what she was saying. She hung up the phone and it rang a second time. She said that the call was from Randy Credico from the *William Moses Fund for Racial Justice.* I had called Randy several weeks before to see if he could help me find out where Isidro had been sent when he was taken from the LSCI (Low Security Correctional Institution), Allenwood. When I said, "Hello," Randy apologized for taking so long to get back to me and asked how my son was doing and how he could help me. When I told him that Isidro had just died, he went crazy. He started ranting and raving and was cursing so loud that I had to move the phone away from my ears. Sanyae asked to speak to him and I overheard her telling him that the Bureau of Prisons intended to cremate Isidro's body.

When I began to protest, she put her hand up and said,

"Let me hear what he is saying." He told her to hold on and that he was going to get an attorney on three-way with us. The next thing I knew there was an official from the coroner's office in Rochester, Minnesota, on the line with us. The attorney gave the coroner his name, told him that he was the attorney for our family and then he told the coroner in no uncertain terms that they were not to cremate Isidro's body. He also told him not to do anything at all until he heard from our undertaker the next morning. After hanging up, he told me not to worry because everything would be alright. I never got to thank the attorney properly because I was so out of it that I never even got his name.

Not knowing what else to do, I began to pace up and down. My mind was racing a million miles an hour. *What was I going to do next?* Then it hit me. I had to tell Isidro's father that he had passed away. He was at work and I figured there was no need to call him at work because he would just be upset during the ride home, and since he was going to be alone, I figured it would be best to tell him when he got there. The least I could do was to let him have the last few moments of peace that he was going to have for a long time. While I was pacing up and down, Sanyae sat down and started making calls, letting everyone know that her brother was gone. I made a mental note to thank her for this later.

Before long, the house was full of people. Everyone who came in would come over to me and hug me very tightly. I don't know where all of these people came from so fast. There were friends, family members, former foster children, coworkers and even some strangers who happened to be friends of my children. With each new group of people, a new floodgate of tears came pouring down. People were offering me food and drinks, but food was the last thing on my mind at the time. I would not be able to think clearly until I completed the most important task at hand and that was to tell Hector that his first-born son had passed away. I was not looking forward to this. I knew that Hector usually got home between 4:30 and 5:30 p.m. and that his mother arrived home shortly after 6 p.m. I figured why not give them a chance to have dinner because it would probably be the last peaceful meal that they would have in a long time.

By 7:30 p.m., I knew I could not delay it any longer and that I would have to go and break the news to Hector. We took two cars and drove off toward his house. When we arrived, we found him sitting outside in the yard smoking a cigarette with his dog, *Shorty*, lying at his feet. He seemed to be enjoying the warm summer night. I arrived in the first car and when he saw me, he smiled and asked what I was doing out of work. When he saw the second car pull up and the girls get out of the car, his smile began to fade and he asked, "Why are you bringing all of these people to my house?" The look in his eyes told me that he already knew the answer to this question.

I walked up to him and put my arm around him, held him tight and said, "Isidro passed away." I could feel his body begin to tremble and the tears from his eyes were mixed with my own tears as they began to roll down the side of my face.

His mother came to the door and as soon as she saw us, she started screaming, "Isidro, Isidro," in her heavy Spanish accent. Before long, everyone standing in the yard was crying with us. Isidro was loved by everyone and now he was gone.

We stayed with Hector and his mother until they both calmed down a little bit and then left after making plans to meet in the morning to begin making the funeral arrangements. When we arrived back at my house, there were even more people there. The news had traveled fast. The phone was ringing constantly and at some point I realized that the ringing of the phone no longer bothered me. For the past few weeks, every time I heard the phone ring, I would get chills and would be afraid to answer it. Now, the ringing of the phone no longer bothered me. It's funny how things in life can change from one minute to the next. At some point, everyone decided that I needed some rest and left so that I could get prepared for the next day. I don't remember getting any sleep, but I do remember lying down for a few minutes and then getting up and pacing up and down for hours smoking cigarette after cigarette. I would use the butt end of one cigarette to light the next one. Before I knew it, the sunlight was streaming through the blinds. I decided to take a long shower so that I would be out of the way before anyone else got up. I then remember that the only other person in the house was Ricky because everyone had gone home late the night before.

After the shower, I got dressed and continued my pacing and smoking while watching the clock. I had a whole hour to go before Hector's mother came to take me to the funeral home. I opened and closed the refrigerator door several times knowing that I should eat, but not being able to. At 8:30 a.m., Hector's mom called to say that she would be there in a half an hour. That would give me time to go to the corner store to get the newspaper, some coffee and a pack of cigarettes. I tiptoed out of the door and closed it softly, knowing that Ricky deserved all of the sleep that he could get because he was going to need it in the days to come. As soon as he saw me, the deli owner asked how my son was doing. Before I could form the words to tell him, I burst into tears and he immediately knew the answer to his question. He seemed sorry that he asked and offered his condolences. I thanked him, took my coffee, newspaper and cigarettes and went home to wait for Hector's mother. When I got in front of the building, I found Lessie, Isidro's daughter, Dee Dee's mother, waiting there for me.

Hector's mother came on time and we rode to the *Porta Celli San German* funeral home in silence. Hector's mother had buried two of her sons at this funeral home and had established a relationship with the director. I was hoping that we were not going to have a problem because Isidro was still legally married, but Hector's mother did not seem the least bit worried and told me that we were not going to have a problem. After parking the car, we went inside and were greeted by *Mr. Lopez* who shook our hands and directed us to his office. He patiently explained that he would have to contact the coroner in Minnesota and make arrangements for Isidro's body to be flown home. I told him what they had said about sending him home in a mid-range casket and government supplied suit. Before he could comment, Hector's mother said, rather loudly and with her thick accent, "Take him out of it. I don't care what they send him in, just take him out of it," meaning the suit and the casket too. I felt the same way. After getting all of the information, Mr. Lopez took us to the back where we chose a white casket to bury Isidro in. Mr. Lopez told me that he would call me when Isidro's body arrived in New York and we left the funeral home. Hector's mother went to work and Lessie and I went back home to make more phone calls and arrangements.

We spent the rest of the morning and early afternoon making phone calls and letting everyone know when the wake and funeral would be. Sanyae and Peanut went to my job and to the projects to put the announcement cards up in the buildings. Whenever someone who lived in the project died, their family would put up announcement cards in all of the buildings. I was so glad that Isidro's funeral was not going to be in the local funeral homes because it seemed like the people in *Edenwald Projects* liked nothing better than a good funeral. A lot of them would go to the funeral home even if they did not know the person who had passed away.

I had always said that when I died, I wanted my funeral to be held in Queens, New York. This way, whoever came to view my body would have to be someone that was close to me during my life and not someone who just did not have anything to do for the night. They were going to have to do a little traveling to get to see Isidro too, because Porta Celli was on the other side of the Bronx.

Somehow I got through the next few hours, but it was not easy. Everyone had been lounging around when Sanyae decided to go into a meltdown state. She started crying really loud and passed out. For the life of me, I will never know how she wound up on the floor in the hallway outside of my apartment, but that is where she was when the ambulance came to check her out. They took her vitals and said that she was fine and then for some reason, they decided to take my blood pressure. I guess I looked a lot worse than I realized. The ambulance attendants told me that my blood pressure was high, but not high enough to be concerned. They also told us to take it easy so that they would not have to come back that night. I guess with all of the drama, time was passing by faster than I realized. Soon it was time for everyone to go home or wherever they were going to be staying for the night. I was not in a hurry to be alone, but I was glad to have a few minutes of peace and quiet.

Shortly before I retired for the night, the phone rang. I just looked at it and wondered who could be calling me at that time of night. I started not to pick it up because late night phone calls always meant bad news to me, but with all that was going on, I decided to answer it. It was Mr. Lopez from the funeral home. He said, "Mrs. Aviles, I picked up your son from the airport." He said it so casually that it was almost like Isidro was still alive. The dam of tears that I had been holding back all day suddenly burst. My son was finally back home in New York, but not the way that I had planned for the seven-and-a-half years. I had always imagined him coming home to a big dinner party like we had when he came home from the Army. I never imagined my son coming home cold and still in a box. I never imagined that his first and last stop upon coming home to New York City would be a funeral home. I fell to my knees and sobbed out loud. Not the kind of sobbing that comes from your mouth, but the kind that comes from the pits of your soul. My boy was home, but I could not hug him and kiss him and tell him that I was glad he made it home. I could not offer him that plate of food that we had talked about all of these years. Instead, I had to get up early in the morning and go and buy him a suit to be buried in. *"God, what have I done in life to deserve this?"* I continued to sob and sob and say, *"Why, why, why?"*

Somehow we made it through the night and the next morning. I got up, showered and got ready to face the day. The first thing I had to do was get a suit in which to bury my son. Sanyae and Danea, one of Isidro's daughter's mother, agreed to take me to Fordham Road to get the suit. We went to several men's stores and looked at several suits. Sanyae seemed to be bargain hunting, which was not fun for me at all. She brought to mind the time I had asked Isidro to take her shopping for some school clothes. They were gone for hours and when he came back, he looked totally stressed out. He said, "Ma, don't ever ask me to take her shopping again." He said that she went from one store to the other trying on this and that. He said after going to almost every store on the avenue, she went back to the first store and bought the first things that she had tried on. He said he had a headache and that he would never take her shopping again. I laughed because that was the very reason I had asked him to take her shopping in the first place. Going shopping with Sanyae was nerve wracking and this day was not different. I finally told her that I was not bargain hunting for a cheap suit to put on my son. Isidro was not the type to put on a cheap suit and I was not going to bury him in one. I went back to the *Porta Bella* men's shop and purchased the white suit that I first saw. Isidro was going to look good in this white suit so I paid for it, took the bag and told them that I was not having fun and that I was ready to go home. Later on, my cousin, Steven, would tell me that I had stepped out into the street in front of the bus that he was driving and that he had to slam on the brakes to keep from hitting me. I don't remember seeing him or the bus.

I asked Sanyae and Danea to please take the suit to the funeral home for me and I went home to try to lie down and get ready for Isidro's wake that evening. I don't know if I had dozed off or if I had been daydreaming, but suddenly I heard knocking on the door. I jumped up and went to answer the door. It was a couple of my friends who had come to help me get through the evening. They immediately sensed that I was dreading going to the wake and advised me to be strong. *How could I be strong when I hadn't even accepted the fact that this was happening?* For seven-and-a-half long years I had hoped that this was just a bad dream and that one day I was going to wake up. Well, I did not wake up and the dream just kept getting worse and worse. We decided that I would not be the first one to see Isidro, but Danea would go in and make sure everything was right before I went in. I waited on pins and needles for her to call back and say that everything was okay. I had been dreading this moment ever since I received the news that Isidro had passed away. Now, I had to wait patiently for them to call and let me know that it was alright for me to come to see my son lying in his casket. All I could think of was how good he would look. He would look handsome in the white suit that I had bought for him. Yes, he would look handsome, but he would not be breathing.

I never got the call from Danea. Evidently she had become very upset upon seeing Isidro laid out. My friend, Betty, called and said that everything was okay, but she was trying to calm Danea down. She said that Danea thought that his hair was too long and had asked the funeral director to cut it down a little. I would have to see for myself. The last time that I saw Isidro in the Mayo Clinic in Rochester, Minnesota, he had a fresh haircut and he was clean shaven. I got ready and headed for the funeral home. As soon as I walked in the door of the funeral parlor, my knees began to get wobbly. I took a deep breath and walked into the room. I put one foot slowly in front of the other until I was finally standing in front of the casket where my first-born child was lying. At that moment, I wanted a casket too. I wanted to die and lie down with him. As I think back on that day, I know it is only the grace of God that got me through. I finally understood what the poem *"Footsteps"* meant. I just stood there staring at my son. He was gorgeous and looked very much at peace which was my only consolation. He no longer looked hungry or hurt and beaten down, but he looked totally at peace. I guess the look of peace on his face gave me the strength to get through the next few days, months and years. But the pain was there. It felt like there was a hole in my chest where my heart used to be. It felt like every time I took a breath, the air would go straight through me.

People started coming from everywhere. I remember a lot of faces and a lot of hugs and kisses and comforting words. I stayed inside as long as I could, but then I began to feel like I was getting smothered with a pillow. It seemed like all of a sudden I felt like all of the air was being sucked out of the room and I rushed to get outside. I rushed out to the front of the funeral parlor and lit the first of the many cigarettes that I would smoke that night. People came from everywhere. There were cops and civilians from several precincts that I had worked with at one time or another. There were neighbors from the projects that I had not seen in so long that I had forgotten that they existed. My aunts and uncles came from everywhere, Long Island, Pennsylvania, Manhattan and upstate New York. There were even a couple of Isidro's fellow inmates who were fortunate enough to have been released. And most of all, there were the girlfriends. They came from all over. There were so many of them that we started trying to keep count. We lost count somewhere around thirty. Isidro was loved by many.

The evening was spent with us going back and forth from the chapel to the outside of the building. I would sit and pray for my son's soul to rest peacefully in heaven and then when I could not take it any longer, I would go outside and smoke a cigarette. At one time I asked the funeral director how much I had owed him. I was surprised that he had gotten Isidro dressed and ready, but he had never once discussed prices with me. When I approached him and asked about the price, he told me to just take my time and that he would discuss it with me later. This was strange because the other funeral directors told us that they would have to be paid in advance before anything could be done at all. I will always be grateful to Mr. Ortiz for this. When he finally told me how much I owed, I did the math in my head and discovered that I was about a thousand dollars short. For some strange reason, I did not panic. My boss at my part time job had told my coworkers to take up a collection for me and whatever they collected, he would match, dollar for dollar. They had done this and when they walked into the funeral parlor, they handed me a card. In addition to this, several friends and family members had given cards to me also. I just sat down in the office of the funeral director and began opening up the cards. When I finished counting the money, I had the one thousand dollars that I needed and then some. I thanked

God, paid Mr. Ortiz and then went back to the chapel so that we could say the rosary for Isidro. After this was done, we all went home to get ready for the final journey for my beloved son. I just kept praying that I could get through the last day without falling apart.

We left the area in several cars and when I got home, there were already several people in my small apartment. There were kids everywhere and they were all making noise and I was about to explode. I just wanted everyone to go home and give me some peace and quiet. I was not ready for a party atmosphere. I asked the children several times to lower their voices. They did not seem to hear me nor did their parents because everyone kept on chatting and laughing as if I had never said a word. My cousin, Gail, said that she had to leave to get ready for the next day. I decided to leave with her and spend the night out because I knew that in my state of mind I would never make it through the night in that noisey house. I grabbed a couple of things, threw them into a bag and told everyone that I would see them the next day.

For some strange reason, I was able to sleep better that night than I had in a long time. After showering and dressing, I headed back to my house. When I arrived in front of the building, there were two limousines and several cars. The sight of the limousines brought home the finality of things and I began to cry. I remembered feeling the same way when the limousine came to pick me up for my father's funeral. In my father's case, he was old and infirm and had lived a long life. In my son's case, his life was cut short when it was just beginning. I started to feel cold and was trembling. I did not want to get into that limousine that was going to take us to my son's final resting place. I wanted to turn around and run in the opposite direction. I tried to appear strong for everyone because the sight of my tears would surely start a domino effect and then everyone would lose control. I cleared my throat and ordered everyone to begin getting their seats in the cars and limos. I said it with such authority that no one dared to challenge me or make any smart remarks.

When we arrived at Porta Celli Funeral Home, the crowd outside parted to let the family into the chapel. That is when everything began to get blurry. I can remember several uniformed officers seated along the south wall of the chapel. They all stood up at attention when we began to file in. We took our seats and the priest came to the podium and began speaking and saying some prayers. While he was speaking, I could hear some people whimpering and moaning behind me. The funeral director came to the front of the chapel and asked everyone to stand and file by the coffin to say their final goodbyes to Isidro. I don't know how I got out of the seat, but I remember two pairs of big arms lifting me up and half dragging me to the coffin. I did not want to go to that coffin and say goodbye to my son. I wanted him to stop playing and get up and go home with me. This was all a terrible joke and it was time to stop. The hands lifted me from the floor and I was standing there looking at my first-born child, telling him goodbye. I started to shake uncontrollably. My knees got weak. I was cold and then the next thing I knew, I was getting out of the limousine again and being dragged into *San Juana De Arco* church. *How did I get here?* My husband was at my side and I could see his pain through the blur of tears that were flowing down my face. We were walking slowly behind a cloth-covered casket. We took our seats and soon we were going for Holy Communion. It was like a movie moving in slow motion. It was a movie and I was in it and this was not the part that I wanted to play.

I found myself standing on a mound of dirt in front of a hole that had been dug in the ground in Saint Raymond's

Cemetery. People were yelling and screaming, "Isidro, Isidro." Others were sobbing, "No, no, no," but all around there was screaming, moaning and crying. One by one the mourners walked up and started gently placing flowers on top of the casket. It was then that I heard the sounds of dirt bike motors roaring in the distance. Isidro loved to ride dirt bikes and I found it ironic that dirt bikes would go rumbling by at this very moment. I took it as a sign from heaven and from Isidro that he was finally alright and that he was back home again. I suddenly bolted from the pair of arms that were holding me and ran up to the casket. I placed my flower on top and said, "Goodbye, my son, I will always love you and I will see you again in heaven. Rest in peace." I then turned around and ran past the limousines to the first car in the long line of cars that had joined the procession and was now parked along the side of the gravesite. I jumped into the first car, which was driven by my coworker, Lisa, and begged her to please get me out of there. I said, "Lisa, please get me out of here, I can't take it another minute." She drove off hurriedly, her tires stirring up dust as we sped through the entrance of the cemetery. I turned toward her and said, "Thank you," and then I asked her not to stop until we were far away from the cemetery.

Lisa and I sat quietly during the ride home from the cemetery. All I could do was look out of the window and think of the finality of it all. My son was gone from me forever. All he wanted to do for the last seven years, seven months and one day was to come home to his family and be a father to his children. Now, that was all taken away from us. No longer could I hug my precious son and tell him that I loved him. I never got the chance to make him that special coming home dinner that I had planned for years. His daughters could never again run to him and jump up into his arms the way they used to do. He would not be there to rent a limousine for them to take them to their proms. He would not sit in the audience during their graduations, and most of all, he would not walk them down the aisle on their wedding day. It was not fair. He had done nothing to deserve this. *Why, why did this have to happen to my son? Was it God's will?* No, it was not. My son was supposed to be here with me. I was full of pain and rage. This was not supposed to happen and I was going to do something about it. As I stepped from the car, I said out loud, to no one in particular, *"The world has not heard the last from me."*

It was a bright sunny day when I looked up to heaven and said, "Son, I will not let your death have been in vain. I promise you that I am going to do something about this, something that will make a change." As I walked into my building, I wondered if I could do better at keeping this promised than I did with the promise that I made to my son on the bright sunny day that he was born. Yes, I was going to keep this promise.

• • •

Dear Isidro,

It has been a long time since I last wrote you although I think about writing you all of the time. Sometimes I think of writing a letter to you and addressing it to heaven and see what happens. Anyway, it has been almost fourteen years since you were first taken away from me and six years since you went home to God. I miss you dearly and think of you every day. There have been several changes since you first went away. When you left home on that fateful day, your oldest daughter, Sidra, was waiting to enter kindergarten. She has now graduated high school and completed a semester of college in Norfolk, Virginia. Laquisha, who was barely two-and-a-half years old, is now in her second year of high school and is doing well despite all odds. Dee Dee, who was in the womb and waiting to be born when you left, is now in middle school. Whenever I look at the three of them, I cannot help but think of how proud you would be of them if you could see them now. Of course, I know that you do see them, but you know what I mean. Your three nieces are also all grown up now. Donya, your oldest niece, is the one that misses you the most. Whenever something goes wrong in her life, she is quick to say, "This would have never happened if Uncle Isidro was here." Donyae is a famous basketball player in high school. She is still as fast on her feet as ever, and Damika is still a beauty queen in training. It has been thirteen years since she first discovered a mirror and she is still as fascinated by her image in the mirror as she was that first day. DeMarco and Dushawn are both nine years old and are as different as night and day. DeMarco is the rough one and Dushawn is the studious one, like his mother. Then there are your two nephews that you never got to meet. First there is Malik, a little ruffian, and then there is the one that was named after you, Isidro. Although Isidro never got to meet you, he talks about you all of the time. When we go to the cemetery, he asks if the headstone is your house now. Sometimes he calls you Jesus. He learned in school that Jesus is in heaven and since I told him that you were in heaven, he figures that you have to be Jesus. He looks at your last picture with the beard and mustache and you can not tell him that you are not Jesus. I guess he has a point, because God is love and now my son, so are you. You also have another niece, Jewell, that was born last July. She is another hell raiser. Whenever I look at any of them, I just wish that "Uncle Isidro" could be here for them.

Although a lot of things have changed since you left, lots of things have remained the same. One of the main things that has not changed is the cruel, inhumane and unjust war on drugs. In the seventies and eighties, there were state and federal laws passed that were supposed to stem the flow of illegal drugs into our communities and make our lives safer, but this has not happened. What has happened is that they have stolen our sons and daughters, mothers and fathers, grandparents and our grandchildren from us and destroyed our families! Another thing that has not changed is that they have taken you, our precious children, and put you into the belly of the new slave ship called prison. They are still using you as a form of free labor for this country. They are still breaking you down mentally, physically and emotionally. As far as I am concerned, there was no reason for you to have been stolen from us in the prime of your life and thrown into the belly of the beast. It served no real purpose for you to spend seven-and-a-half years there only to suffer and die due to lack of medical treatment. One thing you can rest assured of, my son, and that is the fact that I, your mother, will continue to fight the war on drugs until it is won. Since your death, I have been to Albany several times to protest the Rockefeller Drug Laws, I have been to Tulia, Texas, to support the people there who were unjustly imprisoned due to a drug sting, and I have even been to Albuquerque, New Mexico, to speak to Governor Gary Johnson about this drug war. I have also gone to Coleville, Washington, Washington, DC, Philadelphia and several other places to protest this war on our people. And, my precious son, I will continue to do so until all of your brothers and sisters who were incarcerated with you are home again with their families.

So, my precious son, on this, your 40th birthday, the first thing I will do is go to church to pray for your soul to rest in peace. Then, instead of rushing home to begin cooking you one of those big dinners that I have become famous for, I will rush off to the florist to purchase a bouquet of flowers and some birthday balloons that I will place on your grave. It feels so funny when I put those balloons there every year and say happy birthday. I wonder just how happy your birthday could be or would be if you were still here with us. I will stand there and remember different times in your life. One of the times that stands out in my mind was how you always said that you wanted to smell your flowers while you were living. I think of how you loved living in the fast lane— motorcycles, fast cars and fast women. I think about how you used to go horseback riding and scuba diving. It makes me happy to know that you did more in your short twenty-six years than some people do in their entire lifetime. I take comfort in the fact that no one can ever lock you up or take your freedom or spirit ever, ever again. I always thought that you belonged to me, but now I know that God only lent you to me for a short while and now he has taken you back. I would rather have the pain of losing than the loss of never knowing you at all. Isidro, you were a jewel in the crown of my life, my son, and I will love you forever. I will go now, to put the flowers on your grave, sing happy birthday to you and thank God that he chose me to be your mother. Rest in peace, my son, on this, your 40th birthday. Love, Mom.

Fan Mail Page

If you have any further questions, comments or concerns, kindly address your inquires in care of:

Teresa Aviles

At

AMIAYA ENTERTAINMENT
P.O.BOX 1275
NEW YORK, NY 10159

TAviles@FPA.org
or
tanianunez79@hotmail.com

Coming Soon

From
Amiaya Entertainment LLC

"SISTER"
by
Thomas Glover

and

"A ROSE AMONG THORNS"
by
Jimmy Da Saint

www.amiayaentertainment.com

Flower's Bed

Flower's Bed in an incredible tale of a young lady who overcomes her adversities by experiencing pain, understanding reality and surrendering to love. At nine years old, Flower Abrams is as innocent as she was when she was first born. Cared for by both her loving mother and deceitful father, tragedy strikes this young child at an age where teddy bears and lollipops can past for best friends and lunch. Emotionally and psychologically affected by this malicious and brutal attack, flower turned to the one thing that brought her solace...the streets.

Flower's Bed

The Most Controversial Book Of This Era

Written By

Antoine "Inch" Thomas

Suspenseful...Fastpaced...Richly Textured

PUBLISHED BY AMIAYA ENTERTAINMENT

No Regrets

Anthony Wheeler is no different from thousands of poor children growing up in his Bronx housing project. He is being raised by a single mother, as are his two bests friends Dev and Slick, and life for them is as normal as it can be in a housing project under the cloud of violence, drugs and constant murders. But then Anthony goes to visit a relative one day and stumbles onto something that changes his life forever. He is intoxicated by the dreamlike lure of fast money and immediate success that the underworld and drug trafficking offers. He plunges head-on into it and spirals downward to the commission of a crime that could land him in jail for the remainder of his life. Like many of his mates, being in prison forces Anthony to have second thoughts about the path he has chosen. Once the doors clang shut behind him. But, unlike the others, instead of this revelation coming over time, Anthony's metamorphosis happens almost immediately after he is incarcerated. He says he has "No Regrets," but there is a distinctive plaintiveness in the voice echoing in his head about the path he has chosen. He seeks redemption by saying over and over to himself, "Only God can judge me."

From the Underground Bestseller "Flower's Bed"
Author Antoine "Inch" Thomas delivers you

NO REGRETS

It's Time To Get It Popping

"Gritty....Realistic Conflicts....Intensely Eerie"
Published by Amiaya Entertainment

Unwilling to Suffer

Stephanie Manning is a Stunningly beautiful woman with the brains to match her incredible physical gifts. But, with all she has going for her, she has a problemshe's saddled with a husband, Darryl, who can't contain himself in the presence of other beautiful women.

Blinded by love, Stephanie at first denies there was a problem, until one day her husband's blatant infidelity catches up with him, and all hell breaks loose. The marriage crumbles, the couple separates and Stephanie files for divorce, but that's just the beginning of the madness.

Darryl finds himself caught up in more and more bizarre situations with other women while Stephanie tries her best to keep it all together. She is approached by a young thug in the 'hood and becomes engulfed in a baffling sea of emotions as she is drawn into the young man's romantic web.

Will Stephanie's and Darryl's relationship survive, or will Stephanie succumb to the young thug's advances? Find out in this enchanting and engaging story if stephanie is able to avoid being drawn into a world of sex, drama and violence.

That Gangsta Sh!t

That Gangsta Sh!t is an anthology which features "Inch", as well as several other authors. Each author will mesmerize readers as they journey through the suspense and harsh realities that are a few of the reluctant foundations of life. These shocking tales will fascinate, so much that readers won't be able to close the book.

"If It Ain't Rough, It Ain't Right"

THAT GANGSTA SH!T

Featuring Antoine "INCH" Thomas

Shocking...Horrific...

You'll Be To Scared To Put It Down

Published By Amiaya Entertainment LLC

A Diamond in the Rough

A Diamond in the Rough is the compelling tale of Diamond Weatherspoon's life growing up in the ghetto neighborhoods of Brooklyn, NY. Diamond witnesses her mother Angel, who is 15 years her senior, abused and mistreated by her father Rahmel, a womanizer and major player in the lucrative crack game. When Diamond's mother finally summons up the courage to leave Rahmel, she and Diamond are forced to go on public assistance. Already abused and battered in spirit, Diamond and Angel find themselves living in a woman's shelter until the welfare system can find them adequate housing. Diamond's plans of going to college are interrupted and her dreams of a better life deferred.

Shaped by a life of pain and disappointments, Diamond turns to the Brooklyn streets for refuge. Embracing the shiesty lifestyle of the hustlers in pursuit of the easy life, Diamond encounters many types of people. When she meets Shymeek, an up and coming music producer, the dark hell she calls life begins to look brighter. Finally, Diamond has some breathing room. But things are not always what they seem. Life can change drastically at any moment. Journey into the world of Diamond Witherspoon whose story mirrors so many of our young women that are caught up in the chase for a better life. *A Diamond in the Rough* is a stark reminder that in every city neighborhood there is a rough jewel waiting to be polished to brilliance.

A Diamond IN THE ROUGH

JAMES "I-GOD" MORRIS

PUBLISHED BY AMIAYA ENTERTAINMENT, LLC.

I Aint Mad At Ya

Growing up in the mean inner-city streets of Harlem, New York, Freedom, a young black man in his early 20's, learned at an early age how to provide for himself. Growing up fatherless and raised by an ex-dopefiend mother, his options were few. Like so many of his peers, he becomes fascinated by the promise of fast money, power and respect offered by New York's other "business" world.

One day on a humble, Freedom meets Havoc, a Brooklyn native who gets his money by any means necessary. When Havoc takes Freedom under his wing, he introduces him to another world, the art of heisting, murder and mayhem.

Take a sneak peak into a world where violence is normal and betrayal is to be expected. Read and find out if both of these men dodge a destiny of Federal prosecution, prison and death.

TRAVIS "UNIQUE" STEVENS

NY

AVAILABLE NOW FROM
AMIAYA ENTERTAINMENT
ISBN# 0-9745075-5-5

I AIN'T
MAD
AT ya

PUBLISHED BY AMIAYA ENTERTAINMENT, LLC.

All Or Nothing

Anthony "Ant" Fennel was born with the will to survive, by any means necessary. In his world, murder and mayhem are facts of life. In a crucial moment, difficult choices are made and consequences can be severe. Ant comes to understand this harsh reality, as he finds himself incarcerated at the age of 15. After serving 6 1/2 of a 7-1/2 to 15-year sentence in the belly of the beast, Ant knows first hand that when it comes to murder, "One is too many, and a thousand is never enough."

Once released from prison, Ant returns to the infamous life style that had previously consumed him. For a short time he's at the top of the game. But it's truly a lonely place at the top. Murder, madness and money don't make for good friendships. Friends are hard to come by. Who can a brother trust? Are money and the heinous things that come along with it worth the nightmare ride?

Join Ant on his quest to find the answers to these questions and in the process possibly discover the meaning of manhood. See how one young man comes to understand that when it comes to the "game" there is only one rule. Only the strong survive!

ALL OR NOTHING

MICHAEL WHITBY

PUBLISHED BY AMIAYA ENTERTAINMENT, LLC.

Against the Grain

Boo and Moe are brothers who's father died of a drug overdose when they were very young. Raised by a tough mother and her new companion Rufus, the boys grow up to be street-wise, hardened individuals who eventually form their neighborhood's toughest street gang. Toughness was their gang's mantra, and was reflected in their chosen name -- B.M.F., for Bad Mutha Fuckas.

But the brothers were also clever enough to know that all brawn and no brains would eventually spell their doom, so they turned to Rufus for guidance. It was a smart move, because Rufus soon had the rough BMFs drug dealings operating like a well managed organization.

Boo was the brains and Moe was the brawn, and they were a formidable combination that soon was recognized by all the other gangs as top dogs. Boo and Moe owned the streets of their neighborhood.

At this point Johnson takes another turn in his story telling. He makes Boo befriend a young man named Steve who's mother is a heroin addict, and adds another element to Boo's personality by giving him the compassion and the insight to transform himself into Steve's unoffcial mentor. Boo loves Steve so much he asks him to be his newborn son's Godfather.

Everything was fine until Steve brings his cousin Reno into the gang family, and that's when the chaos begins, because Reno is not exactly the sit-back type. Steve soon is caught in the middle of an increasingly deadly power struggle between Boo, Moe and Reno.

Altercations and confrontations occur more frequently each day, so much so that Steve finally admits to himself that he has to make a choice.

At this point, Johnson again adds another twist. Did Boo and Moe think they had enough troubles with Reno? Well, when Boo negotiates with a new drug supplier, here comes one of those rival bad boys from their past who's either jealous or frustrated or both, and off we go again.....

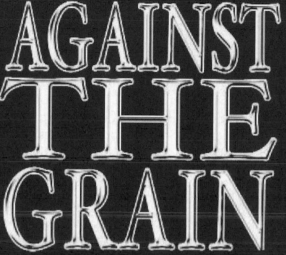

A STORY THAT WILL HAVE YOU ON YOUR TOES FROM BEGINING TO END...

AGAINST THE GRAIN

AVAILABLE NOW FROM
AMIAYA ENTERTAINMENT
ISBN# 0-9745075-6-3

G.B. JOHNSON

PUBLISHED BY AMIAYA ENTERTAINMENT, LLC.

Hoe-Zetta

Hoe-Zetta is the violent off the hook, remorseless, tale of two sexually charged females from the Bronx, NY. Hoe-Zetta was born to a black prostitute mother and a rich white trick father. When her mother Rosette commits suicide, Hoe-Zetta is left all alone in the world. Since her father is unaware of his mulatto infant daughter, Hoe-Zetta is sent off to a group home. Hoe-Zettta finds a best friend in Shanta who also lives at the group home. Together the two burn up Interstate 95 like they were born to be in the game.

Go inside the minds of these two teen-agers who are headed down the wrong path, but determined to succeed by whatever means necessary. This book is unlike anything you have ever read.

HOE-ZETTA

Vincent Warren brings you another "HOT" novel from Amiaya Entertainment

VINCENT "V.I." WARREN

PUBLISHED BY AMIAYA ENTERTAINMENT, LLC.

So Many Tears

ORDER FORM

Number of Copies

So Many Tears	ISBN# 0-9745075-9-8	$15.00/Copy _____
Hoe-Zetta	ISBN# 0-9745075-8-X	$15.00/Copy _____
All Or Nothing	ISBN# 0-9745075-7-1	$15.00/Copy _____
Against The Grain	ISBN# 0-9745075-6-3	$15.00/Copy _____
I Ain't Mad At Ya	ISBN# 0-9745075-5-5	$15.00/Copy _____
Diamonds In The Rough	ISBN# 0-9745075-4-7	$15.00/Copy _____
Flower's Bed	ISBN# 0-9745075-0-4	$14.95/Copy _____
That Gangsta Sh!t	ISBN# 0-9745075-3-9	$15.00/Copy _____
No Regrets	ISBN# 0-9745075-1-2	$15.00/Copy _____
Unwilling To Suffer	ISBN# 0-9745075-2-0	$15.00/Copy _____

PRIORITY POSTAGE (4-6 DAYS US MAIL): Add $4.95

Accepted form of Payments: Institutional Checks or Money Orders

(All Postal rates are subject to change.)

Please check with your local Post Office for change of rate and schedules.

Please Provide Us With Your Mailing Information:

Billing Address_____

Name: _____

Address:_____

Suite/Apartment#: _____

City:_____

Zip Code:_____

Shipping Address

Name:_____

Address:_____

Suite/Apartment#:_____

City:_____

Zip Code:_____

(Federal & State Prisoners, Please include your Inmate Registration Number)

Send Checks or Money Orders to:
AMIAYA ENTERTAINMENT
P.O.BOX 1275
NEW YORK, NY 10159
212-946-6565

www.amiayaentertainment.com